DEATH AT THE END OF A ROPE!

The gallows reared tall. Two nooses dangled, waiting in the hot, high-plains wind.

The wide doors of the jailhouse flew open. The prisoners were marched out by armed committee members, hustled up the scaffold steps, and positioned on the raw pine floor. A parson stroked his copy of the Good Book fussily.

Then the hangman, Zachariah Tree, mounted the gallows steps, a grim sight in his black coat and boiled white shirt, his string tie carefully knotted. Silence gripped the crowd of spectators.

"Any last words?"

The condemned men were tightly pinioned with stout chest, arm, and leg straps.

"Last words?" one prisoner spat. "What in hell for?"

The hangman produced two black cloths from his pocket.

"No objection to hoods, I reckon?" Getting only icy stares for his answer, Tree fixed the blinders in place, then slipped the nooses over the doomed men's hooded heads.

Now even the preacher's mumbling prayer was hushed. The hangman put his right hand on the lever that controlled the traps. He waited a moment, then jerked it down.

The traps dropped quickly, and the culprits fell through the gaping hole, helpless weights.

Dead weights.

QUANTITY SALES

Most Dell books are available at special quantity discounts when purchased in bulk by corporations, organizations, and special-interest groups. Custom imprinting or excerpting can also be done to fit special needs. For details write: Dell Publishing, 666 Fifth Avenue, New York, NY 10103. Attn.: Special Sales Department.

INDIVIDUAL SALES

Are there any Dell books you want but cannot find in your local stores? If so, you can order them directly from us. You can get any Dell book in print. Simply include the book's title, author, and ISBN number if you have it, along with a check or money order (no cash can be accepted) for the full retail price plus $2.00 to cover shipping and handling. Mail to: Dell Readers Service, P.O. Box 5057, Des Plaines, IL 60017.

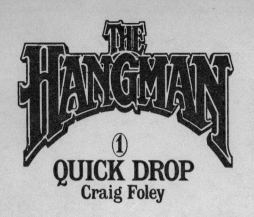

THE HANGMAN

① QUICK DROP

Craig Foley

A DELL BOOK

Published by
Dell Publishing
a division of Bantam Doubleday Dell
Publishing Group, Inc.
666 Fifth Avenue
New York, New York 10103

ISBN: 0-440-20373-2

Printed in the United States of America
Published simultaneously in Canada

July 1989

10 9 8 7 6 5 4 3 2 1
KRI

To Marilyn

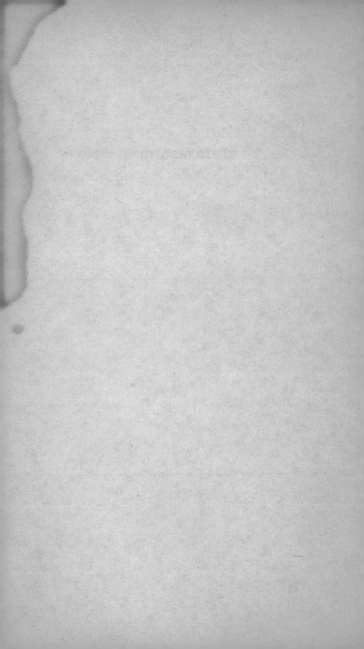

Special Thanks to Charlie Perlberg

Quick Drop

Chapter One

The old-timer and the youth spurred down out of the canyon's mouth, their mounts' hooves thundering on the gravel footing between the vast, tall walls of stone. Soon they were on the flat, the horses running all-out still over belly-deep valley grass as green as the kid's frightened eyes. The "posse" were grinding ground behind them, he sensed, and then there the proof came: a divot exploded in the buckskin bronc's path.

The kid threw a glance over his shoulder to the six riders who were fanning out. Their horses were running fit to burst, flanks heaving, spewing long tails of froth from their mouths. More guns barked, creating a bloom garden of cloud-white smoke puffs. A deadly hail of bullets sang about the heads and straining bodies of the fleeing pair.

1

Was it right to call the hardcase waddies of the Spade Eight spread a posse? the kid wondered. Hell, they were no more authorized by law than a henhouse-raiding coyote.

The old man riding at his side had the same thought racing under the gray shock of hair freed by his blown-off hat. The crime he and his grandson Joe were guilty of was plain, simple homesteading. The valley's biggest rancher hated nesters; that was the reason for today's raid on the soddy by the bank of the stream. It was the reason why this damned chase was another thing that had gone sour, driven into the open on exhausted horses, outnumbered six to two. The old man considered reining in, making a stand, although his and Joe's weapons were a couple of old six-guns and a couple of clasp knives best used for opening wheat-seed sacks. Yet to do just that would be suicide in the open. The waddies would surround them and lob in rifle rounds till they were lifeless, riddled bodies under the high Wyoming sky.

No, there was another chance. A clump of alders and larger cottonwoods stood in the middle of the hill-rimmed flat. It offered protection of a sort: shielding deadfalls, a screen of leaves. The two of them *might* have a chance—if they could make it there. They'd hold the cattlemen off till night, then slip away under cover of dark.

The old man veered the roan he straddled, and the animal lurched in a gallop fraught with stumbling in the direction of the trees. Joe's mount was equally jaded, but the kid spurred on, following his gramp. Now, as the trees and the creek supporting them grew near, they could hear the angry curses from the ranchers.

"Goddamn you nester Pattersons! Catch you, and we'll lynch you sons of bitches! If we don't drill your miserable, farmer carcasses first!"

Bullets spanged between the buckskin's and the roan's pumping legs, but the kid and his gramp were at the margin of the undergrowth now, pushing through brittle sand plum branches. At the creek narrow, the pair reined to sliding halts, and dismounted. "Down behind that cottonwood log! Don't lollygag, lad! Shake a leg!"

The riders of the Spade Eight were in sight atop a looming wave of horseflesh that threatened to engulf them. There was the outfit's ramrod, Sol Pickett, and the ranch owner himself; plump, potato-nosed, mustachioed Phil Larkin, his anger turning his long-jawed, sun-bronzed face into an ugly mask. Both men, like their hardcase henchmen, were bringing rifles to bear, jacking the actions of their oiled, gleaming Winchesters.

"Gone to ground, they have!" the heavyset man called out. "Todd! Armstrong! You boys circle around and we got 'em corralled!"

Larking threw his rifle to his cheek and blazed away, peppering the shrubbery. From the dig-in came a sharp yelp of pain. Then the kid cried, "Gramps! You're hit!"

Rancher Phil Larkin, reining aside his big

3

steel-dust gelding, grinned wickedly at his *seg-undo*. "Time to move in," he grunted, toeing his animal forward. Four riders advanced, staying about ten feet apart, each watchful, long gun at the ready. There was no movement under the trees. For the moment, even the humming wind had dropped.

"We got them nesters now, boss," Pickett snarled, lips taut. "Hunkered like the yellow-bellied cowards they are—"

That was when the crack of the pistol shot cut the midday air. The waddie to Pickett's left gasped and threw a hand to clasp his upper arm that suddenly oozed blood.

"Winged me, by God!"

Larkin whooped, "That tears it! Ride them sons of bitches down! Charge!" All at once the horsemen were in motion, guns barking in a wild fusillade. The kid's buckskin went down thrashing in the brush. Gramps's roan screamed and bolted from cover. A 227-grain ball tore through its eye, and it toppled down, dead. Larkin and his men crashed the brush, continuing to toss shots more or less at random. "There's the one called Joe! Looks like his six-gun's jammed!" Pickett shouted.

Joe knelt beside his wounded grandfather, who was writhing painfully. The young man struggled with scraped-raw fingers at his worn Griswold and Gunnison .36. The old Confederate weapon had failed at the worst possible time.

In an instant, the Spade Eight men had dismounted, even Todd and Armstrong running in from the rear to club the boy. Joe took two stiff blows to the temple but was nevertheless up and fighting back. His slouch hat askew on his towhead, he threw himself at the attackers, launched a punch at Larkin, but was blocked by Todd. Todd kneed him hard in the groin, and the kid folded like a dropped concertina.

The hardcases crowed around Joe and Old Matt Patterson and began kicking and stomping in a slow, deliberate fashion. Leaving the kid to the waddies, Bossman Larkin and Pickett, the hulking giant, stood over old Matt. The grandpa's bullet-drilled side pumped a spurting stream of blood, but he was far from dead. In fact, judging from the location of the red stain on the shirt of frayed calico, the old-timer, given proper treatment, might recover, walk a plowed field again, and breath the sweet perfume of the soil.

The ranch owner's mouth twisted beneath his mustache. He peered down at the groaning old-timer and sneered. "You was warned to clear outta these parts, you old fart. You squatted on the Spade Eight range; land I killed a passel of Arapaho to gain and hold. Sure, that happened years ago, but the land's still mine."

" 'Tain't," Matt Patterson managed to bite out. His side felt skewered on a spit of flame, and it took all his strength to talk. "Th' homestead law, it says—"

"You got nerve to bring that up on the day you'll swing from a noose, like I swore to m' boys. You and that grandson. Appears to me you need more humbling!" With that, he dug a bootheel into the soft black loam, raised his other foot, angled his ankle to poise a long-roweled silver spur. He lowered the sharp rowel points slowly into the helpless man's crazed eyes, then drove down, dragging the spur rowels across the old man's weathered cheek, implanting a row of tiny, crimson-beaded punctures. Patterson squirmed and yowled, so Pickett kicked him roundly to the chin. Patterson slumped unconscious, his head limp in the grass.

"Tie the nooses," Phil Larkin Barked, and a couple of waddies moved to where their mounts stood. They took the lariats from their saddle pommels and eagerly brought them back. The breeze had picked up again, and the swaying tree branches threw patterns of shadow overhead. A mockingbird called out.

"Damn, but this'll be fun!"

"First th' older, and the t'other! So's we can see how the younger takes Gramp's air dance!"

"The big cottonwood will do," Larkin said. Pickett nodded and the other hardcases grinned.

From his position huddled on the ground, Joe Patterson just stared. This couldn't be happening, his brain roared over his hurt. Not to Gramp! Not to me! He tried to scramble up.

"Hold it! Don't move!" The man called Armstrong, skinny but tough, jammed a Colt Navy

Model under Joe's bloodied nose. The muzzle looked like a yawning cave. Joe subsided.

By this time, Armstrong and Pickett had thrown a rope end over a stout bough of the big tree. Todd and his pard were leading up a stocky bay that was shedding off its coarse winter hair. Both homesteaders' broncs lay stiff and stinking.

"Thataway, Ears. Give us a hangman's knot, like you learned in prison." Ears, so nicknamed because his were so big, elongated, and hair tufted, was a homely, clumsy man. He toiled busily, and at last his noose turned out. Larkin signaled, and two men dragged old Patterson to his shaky feet. His face was a sheet of blood now, but he was awake enough to struggle as his wrists were bound.

"No!" Matt Patterson moaned.

"You aim to beg, nester?"

"Not for my own life, but the lad's. He's just sixteen and—"

"Never done no one harm?" Behind Larkin's back, a rumble of laughs erupted.

"That's c'rect!"

"Palaver is time wasted, old man. The kid swings the same as you! Sol!"

"Yeah, boss?" Pickett said.

"Take over. And make it slow."

The final preparation didn't take long, and soon the old-timer sat propped for his last ride. The horse under him danced about nervously, spooked by the general excitement. Pickett slipped the noose over Patterson's head, then

7

drew the knot tight at his stubbled, quivering jaw. The intended victim trembled now from top to toe, and the split lips mumbled a few simple prayers.,

The wiry Armstrong jabbed Joe's ribs with the Colt's barrel. "Eyes open there! Else we make it worse for 'im!"

"Whip up the bronc!" Phil Larkin shouted, shaking his fist. There was the urgent thud of hooves as the animal jumped ahead. Matt Patterson, aged and withered as an autumn leaf, was yanked backward from the saddle by the tautened rope. His eyes bulged as he swung, pendulumlike. A roaring gurgle burst from his contorted lips.

Joe knelt down, frozen. His howl of anguish rang on the warm Tetons wind. Tears streaked the kid's blanched cheeks.

The hanged man jerked and twitched hideously. His face swelled and purpled. He was strangling, and as he choked he twisted and kicked. Patterson's bladder and bowels emptied in a stinking rush.

"Haw," laughed fat Phil Larkin, his jowls and cannonball belly shaking.

Zachariah Tree heard the strange cry and drew rein on his leggy black gelding. The wail of a coyote-trapped jackrabbit? he wondered. No, a human sound, a damned *pitiful* human sound, if he'd ever heard one. And he *had* heard plenty in his time, God knew.

He sat high on his mount in the middle of a meadow blooming with buttercups, straining to hear more. Behind was the notch he had just ridden through; beyond, the valley of peaks white with unmelted snow. Tree was a man near forty, just middling height, but powerfully built, with shoulders that bulged beneath his shirt. His face was lean, with strong features, hidden under a black Stetson. His nose sniffed the wafting air and caught the faint scent of gunsmoke.

"Ahead there, horse," he muttered. "That bit of woods along the creek."

Another yell drifted across the flat: "No, don't string me up, too! No!"

Zachariah Tree's gray eyes sharpened as he heard the cry, and he kicked the horse into a shambling run, cursing. His big hand fisted his Colt's handle as he drew the weapon. The black's hooves drummed wildly as Tree drove it harder into the dense shrubbery and up to the stream bank.

There stood six brawny figures wrestling with a towheaded kid. In the background, suspended from a branch, swung a lynched man, his face bloated, his neck stretched, and his swollen tongue protruding. And the poor bastard's agony went on and on. The frail body still convulsed, the spindly legs moved in jerky little circles.

"Hold it!" Tree shouted, although he knew full well. The men on the ground whirled, clawing for their shooting irons.

9

"Try and stop us, mister—"

Tree's Colt bucked in his hand. A bullet exploded the skull of the hardcase named Todd, and he pitched violently into the water and sprawled still. Simultaneously, the rest of the crew opened fire. Tree spun and triggered again, this time throwing a shot at the man with the big ears. This fellow was drilled through the breastbone, flinging his Winchester in the air as he crumpled like a wet sack and dropped by the feet of his mustached boss.

"Th' jasper's backing the nesters!" the bossman whooped. "Ventilate him good!" All up and down the line of men, weapons shot lead and smoke. The kid had broken free and, scooping up a fallen pistol, joined in with the newcomer. With slugs zipping past like angry hornets, the man in black wheeled his mount to deal hot lead. A leg-shot waddie crouched and leveled his gun barrel at the horse.

The kid stopped him with a shot that plowed in below his belt buckle and hurled him down, writhing in bloody pain. A long string bean of a hardcase drew a bead on his pard's killer, but Tree's .45 opened up his chest.

"Christ! Pickett!" Larkin shrieked. "Armstrong, hold 'em off!" He heaved his bulk around clumsily, and made for his horse. As he brushed past Matt Pattersons still-jerking form, his shirt got smeared with the victim's excrement.

"Damn you, Larkin!" Armstrong, fleeing, too, overtook the stouter man and leaped for the nearest mount. The bossman swung aboard the nearest bay and gave hard spur. Men and mounts rocketed out of the small glade followed by a rain of the kid's bullets. Inside a minute the riders were out across the flat, galloping full out, panicked and defeated.

The rush of quiet after the booming volleys left Tree's ears ringing. Now that he was able, he urged the black to where the lynched man swung, drew a knife, and used it to slash the tough rope above the noose. Catching the body as it sagged with his left arm, he gently lowered to the ground. Stepping from leather, he knelt for a look-see. After what the victim had been through, there wasn't much that he—or anyone—could do.

"Is he . . . Is he alive?" The kid's voice was like the whisper of crunched corn husks.

"No." Tree climbed slowly to his feet.

Now the kid lay stretched flat, his head to his gramp's thin chest. "But I heard a heartbeat! Maybe if we give him water . . ." Strong, blunt fingers worked at where the lariat strands were embedded in the neck, and the skin parted to expose torn tendons.

"Won't do no good, boy. I've seen it before lots of times. A feller meets his end by hanging, his heart'll keep going a spell. Sometimes as much as ten minutes."

A fresh welling of moisture ran from the towhead's eyes. "Th-they claimed he wouldn't feel nothing."

"The old-timer felt plenty. They always do,

swung off a horse from a branch or pole. Without the jerk of a long drop, they choke to death. Bad for onlookers, worse for the culprit."

"My gramps, he weren't no culprit!" The kid reared up from the finally still form, and peered at Tree curiously. "Say! You sure know scads 'bout hanging and such. And you don't look like no hardcase feller as had come out of prison."

The man clothed all in black said nothing; just waited.

"Look, mister," the kid went on. "I'm Joe Patterson and this dead man is my gramps. Though I wish you mighta got here sooner, I am plumb grateful that you saved my bacon. Mind if I ask who you are?"

"Don't mind." The man was solemn, as he usually was at times of introductions. His gray eyes gazed into the kid's with calm compassion. What had happened to young Joe's gramps hadn't been a miscarriage of justice, but pure, plain injustice, as lynchings without trial always were. "I know so much about dying and executions on account of I'm a hangman, Joe. I work inside the law, not like those lynchings. Obliged to meet you." He thrust out his hand. "The name's Zachariah Tree."

Chapter Two

Joe Patterson decided to bury his grandfather in the hills where they'd often fished together, and enlisted Zack Tree's help. As they strapped the old man's body to one of the Spade Eight cow ponies, the kid said, "Yeah, I'm afeared to go back to the homestead. Larkin and his boys'll get around to going back there. Ain't no future for me in these parts, nohow." He cast gloomy eyes on the other dead jaspers, then looked at Tree.

The hangman shrugged. "They brought what they got on their own selves. Ain't no kin of ours. And I reckon the rancher feller'll want to plant them over to the spread's grave plot."

"Then we can ride off, and just leave 'em."

"The sooner, the better. I got a train to flag tomorrow on the U. P. main line."

Joe frowned. "Twenty miles south. You'll make it, easy. Got a hanging?"

Tree nodded. "Place called Red Bluff."

"Well, I'm heading back for Sandusky. Had me enough of Wyoming Territory."

They mounted and rode out, Joe straddling a tough Spade Eight bronc. Tree sat awkwardly in the saddle, one hand behind, steadying a traveling bag that he'd tied on.

"What's in the big black leather case?"

"Clothes. My equipment."

That shut the kid up, and they trotted side by side in silence for a good long while. At last the ground started to slope and steepen, and a bit later the broncs moved along under pines. "Not much farther now," Joe said.

Tree nodded.

"You say you work for the law?"

"That's right. Capital punishment's legal in this country for murder and treason. Somebody's got to carry out the guilty verdicts." He turned in the saddle and glanced across at the kid.

"You really do to men day in and day out what them bastards done to my gramps."

"Not hardly. I don't kill for orneriness or to steal what belongs to others. And I don't deal in torture, neither. But I don't need make no excuses to you, boy."

"No offense, Mr. Tree. I'm beholden. There's the spot I thought to bury Gramps, yonder under that ridge. It won't rain so hard on him there, you see."

"I see."

After they'd heaped the stiffened body with rocks, Tree fished in his shirt pocket for the makings. He sprinkled Union Leader tobacco from the small sack into the rolling paper, and built a passable quirly. The kid didn't want to smoke, but he had more questions as the older man fired up. "I wonder what it's like, being a hangman. I recall when I was little, before Ma and Pa died, there was a hanging in our town, and they wouldn't let me go. Found out afterward there was a big crowd—thousands. Folks even watched from steamboats on the river. Three men swung on the same gallows, and there was nary a kick or squirm out of any. And the hangman was thought a hero, and had drinks bought for him after in the tavern on the green."

Tree grunted and eyed the sun overhead. "It can be that way. These days, citizens like a public hanging. Seems to give them a thrill *I* can't see."

Joe Patterson's immature face wrinkled in distaste. "People got to be a mite loco. Say, did I hear right? That a hangman'll string up a female same as a man?"

"If she's been found guilty of cold-blooded murder and sentenced by a judge. But it ain't quite the same as for a man. Men take a rope of five strands, women four."

"Gosh, Mr. Tree."

Tree was going to have to be on his way. The nag he'd bought cheap up in Helena for this trip was rested, and should easily make it to the Union Pacific right of way. Then Tree could resume his usual means of travel—trains.

"Son, killing's always dirty, legal or not. Plenty folks hate my guts for doing my job, not just kin and *compadres* of them that's swung."

"Sounds like one hell of a life."

"Son, it is."

Smoke billowing, wheel noise racketing, the diamond-stacked locomotive charged across the prairie. A whistle blast sliced the sun-shimmered air with a pulsing roar. Zachariah Tree stood on the embankment watching the approach, waving his flagged bandanna for all he was worth. Closer, closer . . . and the rapid chuff-chuff gained a distinct rhythm; the rails beside him shuddered and sang. Sand poured from the engine onto the track, and there was a harsh screech as braked flanged wheels bit the sand.

The Union Pacific Line's westbound flyer slowed until it stood stock-still against the backdrop of the distant Wind River Range. A burly brakeman shouted from atop the tender, and a conductor swung to the ground back down the row of cars. Tree plucked up the reins of the tethered black and led it to the staked stock car just as the ramp was thrust down. It was the work of a few minutes to load the animal, then ascend an end platform, pay his fare, and make his way to a vacant seat next to a window. Couplings clanked and steel squealed against steel. They were under way.

Tree leaned back and put off rolling a quirly, looking out at the day, the countryside. He held a fondness for Wyoming Territory, far as it was from his native Texas. The mountains and wide empty plains—the more unsettled an area was, the more he felt at home. Less commotion, less need for killing.

Born and raised in the West, Tree had never considered living anywhere else. He knew it was a raw, harsh land, even aside from natural dangers. It was a land rank with lawlessness—no, that wasn't *quite* corect. Laws existed, all right, but they were too often difficult to uphold. Enforcement trailed the need to punish outlaws. Officials were sometimes helpless, and jails far off. Lynchers slayed without benefit of trial, and many innocent men and women were hanged. Tree did his part to tame the country by joining the profession of a legal hangman.

A pretty young lady left her seat and walked up the aisle of the rocking, rattling car. The full skirts of her apricot silk dress brushed the elbows of the passengers. Finally she had made her stumbling way to a point opposite Tree. She gave a lighthearted smile. "The gentleman where I was sitting has lit a foul cigar, I'm afraid. Would you mind awfully, sir, if I took this empty place?"

"No, ma'am." Tree lifted his bulky traveling bag to make more room for her.

"Oh, thank you. I couldn't have stood it

where I was another minute." She squeezed the skirts and her trim self into a comfortable position, then tossed her brown curls. "I'll try not to be a bother."

"No bother, ma'am."

"Oh, since we'll be riding together, why not call me by my name? Henrietta Dobkins."

"Pleased to make your acquaintance, Miss Dobkins. Zachariah Tree."

Her eyes were wide as china saucers and green as the sea. "Zack. That's a nice name. Friendly seeming. But use Henrietta to me, won't you, please?" She leaned forward to adjust her shoe. Round breasts as white as snow and smoother than satin bulged above her low-cut, lace-filled neckline, and it was all that Tree could do to hold in the returning grin he longed to give her. He knew the daughter of a respectable, genteel family when he saw one, even though she might be a bit impulsive, in love with the notion of making eyes to a male stranger, seeing where it all could lead.

"Very well, then. Henrietta."

"My daddy is a Sacramento newspaper publisher," Henrietta Dobkins purred. "Where are you from, Zack?"

"Down Texas way. Little cow town on the Trinity River." Somehow, for a change, he didn't mind discussing his past so much. Not with this fresh-faced gal. Maybe when the Red Bluff job was done, he'd make some free time and go and visit Sacramento. . . .

A butcher boy vendor plied the aisle, offering

apples and sandwiches for those with hunger pangs. Tree had other fish to fry, and seemingly, so did the woman. When the interruption was past she batted her long lashes and spoke in her most confidential tone, honey sweet, seductively pitched. "You know, Zack, I've got the busiest inquisitive streak, and I just wasn't brought up to be shy with questions. Will you satisfy my curiosity? What do you carry in that great big, shiny satchel?"

"I don't mind saying, since you ask. It's my work kit, Henrietta. A five-strand rope, a four-strand rope in coils. Straps for pinioning on the scaffold—"

"My God!" Henrietta Dobkins's sweet face soured and suddenly went pale and chalky. The bright teeth disappeared as her mouth formed an O. Her small hands wrung her reticule like a sopping dishrag.

"Henrietta?"

"Rope? Scaffold? Don't play with me, Zachariah Tree! Trying to disgust me, as if you were a hangman! It isn't funny!"

"Damned right, it ain't funny! Legal hanging is a serious business."

"Oh!" Henrietta Dobkins stood up so abruptly that she entangled her dress hem in one of the brass buckles on the flap of Tree's traveling bag. As the young woman twisted and tugged, her face grew redder and redder. People in nearby seats turned their heads to stare at her, and a drummer in a suit actually rose to lend assistance. But no assistance was needed, for she yanked free and fled headlong in a huff to the rear of the car through the door leading to the observation platform.

The drummer cast glaring eyes on Tree, but sat back down, thinking better of speaking to the man in black. Within a few minutes, the other passengers, too, were back to minding their own business.

Tree shrugged, pulled out the sack of Union Leader, and built the smoke. As he fired up, the fleeting flame gave him a thought, and he chuckled inwardly.

Hope the sparks from the engine's stacks don't scorch your dress out there, Henrietta Dobkins. You want to look good, stepping down off the train in Sacramento. Catch the attention of an eligible politician dude.

The sun was well westerned when the blue-uniformed conductor pushed through from the car ahead. "Red Bluff a-comin' up," he called. "A half-hour stop or so whilst we take on water! Ladies and gents can eat a bite at the depot cafe. Th' next stop's Red Bluff!"

Tree wrapped his big left fist around the handles of his traveling case. It was his habit to always keep his gun hand free, just in case. He'd made enemies during his nine long years in the hangman's trade, and one or more could turn up when he least expected it.

And besides, he was likely to make a whole new slew of enemies in Red Bluff, wasn't he?

It always seemed that was the way things went.

* * *

A town built up straddling the transcontinental line's main track, Red Bluff had all the usual features of a new railroad town, and maybe some extra thrown in for good measure. Zachariah Tree jumped down from the day coach's step to the platform just as the train rolled to a halt. He'd need to talk to the station agent about the horse that would be unloaded, but first he paused amid the crush of restaurant-bound passengers to survey the freshly painted depot, the hard-packed street, and buildings in various stages of completion. Despite all the construction, the town still looked shabby. But then, he'd seen worse.

Now, as the blush of sunset colored the sky over the peaks, lamps were being lit in windows along the main drag flanking the tracks. Casting a glance to his left, Tree glimpsed the darkened section yard kept up by the U. P., filled with piled ties, stacks of rails, fishplates, and the like, for track maintenance. Once done inside the depot, there was no doubt of the direction he should head in.

Exactly twenty minutes later, by his pocket Waterbury watch, Tree emerged into the deep dusk, sauntering with his bag in hand. There was a jerry-built hotel which he'd bypassed, figuring to do better later at a rooming house, since he planned to spend three or more days. He eyed a chophouse ruefully, but knew his first stop had better be to see the local law. The name

21

he'd been given was that of Sheriff Cain Van Aalst, in whose jail the man he'd come to hang was being held.

The condemned was a young local by the name of Ben Whitlow; a small rancher till he'd apparently joined an outlaw gang to raise his prospects. A month back he'd been convicted of robbing the express car of a train. Three guards had been shot dead by the gang, the rest of whose members had gotten away. Whitlow had been tracked down by a dauntless railroad detective, and that was all that Tree knew about the case.

A good thing about being a hangman was the fact that he didn't need to know the case at all. Catching offenders was the chore of others in the justice system, as was trying the accused, obtaining guilty verdicts, and pronouncing sentence. Only when a duly authorized judge handed down a death sentence were Tree's skills brought into play.

He'd often thought it a relief, of sorts, to no longer be a lawman himself. Tree had spent time working as a deputy down in Texas under his sheriff father. Well, it had been a long time ago.

Tree never minded the life-and-death risks of being a dedicated lawman—he had courage enough for ten. But after what had happened outside old Fort Parker to his father . . .

Tree was striding past an opulent saloon called the Bijou, the raucous noise of music and shouts drifting over the bright red bat-wings, as he spotted the stark, bare-bones framework looming in the street beyond: Red Bluff's under-construction, spanking-new gallows. It stood in front of a low stone structure bearing the sign Jail in big, bold letters.

Entering without knocking, Tree closed the door after him, taking in with a cool glance the wall of wanted dodgers, the locked gun case, and the chipped oak desk. There were two ladder-back chairs on one side of the hall that led back to the lockup. One chair was occupied. The sheriff scowled up at the visitor.

"This had better be important. I was aiming to go out for supper."

"Supper's important. So's meeting a feller come four hundred miles."

"Then you're not my jurisdiction, mister." The badge packer heaved up his considerable bulk, snatched a wide-brim from the hat rack. Two steps started him across the floor, but then Tree blocked his lurching path.

"To perform a hanging." It was all it took. The sheriff's expression changed from harassed to surprised. He stopped trying to shove past the man in black, working his thick lips like a landed trout.

"You're Zachariah Tree? The hangman sent for by the town committee?"

"Tree's my name, all right."

"Then you're welcome as a slim thigh on a dollar whore! Red Bluff's expecting you! Drop that suitcase and take a load off them famous feet."

Tree knew bullshit when he heard it. "My feet are famous, are they?"

"Oh, not well-knowed like them hands, maybe—a real rope man's hands—haw! Say, just a minute!" He scuttled into the back corridor, shouted toward the cells. "Yo, Whitlow! The hangman's come to town! Start saying your prayers! Haw!" Only then did the round, jowled face turn to appraise Tree. "Oh, yeah. I'm Cain Van Aalst, Tree, sheriff of the country roundabout." He dropped back in his chair, crossed his legs with a flourish, slammed the hat on the desk top. "So . . ."

There was a moment of uncomfortable silence. Tree hadn't missed Van Aalst's cruel streak, noting that he'd announced his arrival to the condemned with a sneer and a laugh. Finally Tree remarked, "I figured I'd best let you know I just got off the westbound, sheriff, was safe in Red Bluff and ready to go about my duty. Now you're all told, if you've got supper or some other appointment on order, we can talk about the details in the morning."

Sheriff Cain Van Aalst seemed to have lost his sense of rush. He was almost leisurely now, drumming blunt fingertips, fidgeting with his star, looking around the lamplit office as if trying to decide just what had to be done next. "Thing is, we in Red Bluff are mighty anxious to get Ben Whitlow out of a cell and sent down to hell, where murderers go. He's the worst kind, you understand. Won't admit nothing, claims he's innocent as a newborn babe. Only trouble

24

with his story, though, it don't hold water. Justin Boyle, he followed Whitlow's mount's tracks from where the train was robbed straight to the Whitlow spread. Arrested the feller, brung him to town. The trial was quick but fair, the verdict being that the son of a bitch is guilty."

"Justin Boyle, he's the railroad dick?"

Van Aalst picked his nose and wiped the harvest on his twill trousers. "That's c'rect."

"I reckon he found the stole money at the Whitlow place?"

"No, that's all gone, took by Ben's sidekicks on the raid. Had to've been that way."

"Likely." Something unexplained about the business. Tree felt a familiar itch starting to grow in his mind. "Sheriff, looks to me like—"

But there was no chance for Tree to speak his piece because just then the outside door sprang open at a violent kick. An older jasper plunged across the threshold, his tobacco-streaked white beard wagging like a sheep's tail, and a fisted Bowie knife appearing a lot less cheerful a sight. This old-timer launched himself at Tree with a gurgle and a roar, kicking aside the spittoon on the floor next to the desk. Tree, leaping up, slipped in the slimy spill and went to one knee. "Word's around town," the bearded man half shrieked. "Come to hang my Ben, you rotten hangman bastard!"

"Christ," Van Aalst rumbled. "Whitlow's pap! Tree, watch your ass!"

Tree, seeing the blade coming, dodged side-long and slipped again.

"Die you own self, hangman bastard!" The old man had a seamed face, brown as a nut from outdoor living. Past his prime, he was still tough and wiry, and his slitted eyes seethed with a crazy light.

The knife came up and over in a quick, tight arc at Tree's neck.

Chapter Three

Zachariah Tree threw his body into a roll to avoid his attacker, but out of the corner of an eye glimpsed the crazed old man diving with his knife. The gleaming, sharp blade flashed downward and took a small slice off the hangman's sleeve, then drove into the boards. With a curse he jerked it loose and tried again to stab his quarry, but by now Tree was in a position to grab his arm, wrest it back, and slam it against the desk. The weapon didn't drop, though. This was one determined gray-beard coot. Whitlow fell on Tree, his knee aimed for a groin blow, but missed narrowly, the hangman clinging to him.

"Polecat! Goddamned crooked law!" It was a breathless croak, for the old-timer's energy was failing. Still he remained a dangerous opponent as long as he hadn't lost the knife. He knew it.

Tree knew it. Tree heaved upward with an arched back and hurled the aged Whitlow away from him and into the wall. However, with more foolhardiness than good sense, the old man kept up kicking, scratching, and fighting. The arm locked in Tree's iron grip strained hard. Spittle flowed over toothless gums and onto the ragged hickory shirt.

Tree, a man conditioned as well as any by a vigorous life spent out of doors, sprang up and at old Whitlow with his powerful right arm cocked for a lightning blow. A strong swing with his free arm carried the old man half-around, letting Tree slip close. His fist shot out, hammered the white head above the ear, felling old Whitlow like an ax-chopped pine. He caromed off the corner gun cabinet, his eyes glassy, pitched to the floor, and was still. Zachariah Tree stood over him and slowly unballed his clenched hands. He kicked the knife over toward the gaping Van Aalst.

"Sheriff, you sure ain't one to back a feller."

The lawman licked his lips. "Weren't me old Caleb had his sights set on. I took his shooting iron earlier. Seems he was riled and getting liquored up."

"Well, that's something, leastways." The hangman straightened his frock coat and gun belt. "This is the condemned man's pa? I can see he don't cotton to the guilty verdict. Why'd he call us 'crooked law,' anyway?"

"Damn you, Cain Van Aalst," came a holler from down the lockup. "I heard the ruckus!

What'd you and your hangman do to my paw?"

"Shut up, Whitlow," Van Aalst shouted over his shoulder.

There was a crash of what sounded like a tin bucket against stout bars. The racket was constant, overpowering a string of curses.

"I better get back there before he breaks something. You coming?" Tree followed back along the cells. He'd have to meet the condemned soon. Now was as good a time as any.

There were four barred cubbyholes in the building's rear, paired together on either side of the narrow aisle. Conveniences were short; each held a cot, a slop bucket, and no more. The place stank of sweat, stale urine, and rotten food: the same odors of a hundred jails Tree had visited for duty's sake.

Whitlow was the only prisoner. A man in his early twenties, slender of build, with untrimmed hair the color of crisp, raw carrots, he wore ordinary clothes, a gingham shirt, and twill pants. His belt had been taken, as were his boots. At the moment, he was determined as could be to raise hell.

The din in the narrow quarters sounded like a thousand and a half dropped anvils as the condemned man clanged his empty bucket across the bars. Sheriff Van Aalst simply ignored it all as he strode up, swept a large ring from a chain hooked beside his holster, and unlocked the cell door with a thick key. Within seconds he was inside with the prisoner. For all the hesitation the lawman had shown toward interfering in Tree's tussle with the old man, now he moved with swift decisiveness. His hand came up from his waistband, clutching a sawed-short piece of wheel spoke, and jammed the rounded end sharply in the troublemaker's solar plexus. Ben Whitlow doubled over with a wracking gasp. The sheriff raised the club and brought it powerfully down on the back of Whitlow's skull.

The man went rigid, then his knees buckled as if turned to jelly. The noise when he hit the floor was a soft thud.

"There. That'll teach you." Van Aalst toed the unconscious fellow over on his back and scowled down at him. "Some kind of welcome you give our well-knowed visitor."

"Don't know as I blame the feller much, though," Tree said from beyond the bars. "Ain't met but few since I been in this business who was glad to meet the man brung to put them to death."

The sheriff cocked a curious eye. "Some were glad?"

"Mostly them as got shot up bad getting captured after their crimes. Once in Nevada there was a crazy gutshot Mexican." He looked the crumpled form over. "What do you know about Ben Whitlow from before his arrest, Sheriff? Raised in these parts? He ever break the law before?"

"No." Van Aalst came through the door, stepping toward the front in his heavy shamble, and used his key to lock up. "But there's always a first time to show a bad seed. That's what Boyle pointed out at the trial. Makes sense."

"Justin Boyle testified?"

"Star witness. A good talker. Hell, a damned good tracker, too."

"He led the posse that picked up the bandits' trail?"

Van Aalst stopped and fixed Zack Tree with a stare. "Just Whitlow's trail. And there weren't no posse along that day, just the railroad detective on his own. Why?"

Tree shrugged. "Curious. Say, you want me back when the feller comes around?"

"Tomorrow'll be soon enough."

"Then, I'll just find me a room somewheres around town. Help you drag the old-timer to a cell?"

"Good idea." He stepped around the corner and into the office. "Hey! What the son-of-a-bitching—"

Now Tree saw what had happened, too, coming up behind the lawman. The office was empty. All that remained of old Caleb Whitlow was the door he'd left open.

First engage himself a room, Tree decided, then go looking for the best cafe supper he could locate on short notice. Last would come the bath he needed to get the combination of trail dust and train soot off his skin and out of his dark sorrel hair which had grown long at the nape. He trudged the boardwalk along Red Bluff's main street, still lugging the heavy traveling bag.

He'd left the sheriff's office in a hurry once it grew clear that Van Aalst's mood had turned mean. He'd actually seemed embarrassed that old Caleb Whitlow had run off after the fight, had been given the chance thanks to the diversion created by the son.

Now Tree left behind the more brightly lit district of the town and passed by the last seedy dry-goods emporium and the final whorehouse, with its lit red lantern in a front window. Off to his left lay the helter-skelter mass of frame houses connected by footpaths—the citizens' dwellings. In the maze he would either find a place that took lodgers or he wouldn't find one. He kept his eye peeled for a sign. Sometimes they were modest and hard to spot.

The place reminded him of Vermilion, Texas as it had been when he'd returned to it from the war: it was a balmy spring evening, the scent of cooking on the breeze, a barking dog in the distance.

Zachariah Tree closed his mind to the notion and picked up his pace. The other was a time when his father had been alive. The world had looked a good deal better then to the young man with the bright, new deputy's star. He'd expected the bad killing to end with Lee's surrender over at that place called Appomattox in Virginia.

Except it was only when he got home that the

killing come close to home. His only living kin . . .

Suddenly, he saw the small, white sign carefully lettered in what, he had no doubt, was a feminine hand. Rooms to Let. He turned up the path and mounted the three steps to the whitewashed porch. Two raps, and the door was opened.

"Yes?"

The woman looked a bit older than Tree. Her dark hair, worn in a bun, was streaked with gray, and her bow-shaped mouth was bracketed by a few slight lines. The form under the dress and apron, though, was fine, full bosomed, and small waisted. "I'll be staying in town a few days," he told her. "I need a room. I like the appearance of your place."

"Yes, I rent rooms. And I have a vacancy—several, in fact. You may as well know, mister, I'm a bit new in this business. Lately widowed."

"Sorry."

"Thank you. Won't you step in?" Tree needed no further invitation, and in a minute he was standing on a worn but clean rug. The parlor was lit by a lamp with a stained-glass shade. That was the only expensive-looking piece. The rest was old fruitwood tables, old horsehair settees, and an ancient wood stove, now cold and unlit. "My sleeping rooms are fifty cents a night. Would you care to see one?"

"Not necessary, ma'am, I'm sure one will do. But I want you to realize what you'll be in for. My name's Zachariah Tree. I'm—"

She smiled a tiny, tight smile. "Mr. Tree, I've heard of you. You're the hangman, come to do for Ben Whitlow. Red Bluff's awaited your arrival."

"If you mind a hangman's rooming in your house—"

"Mind? Of course not. I'm Ann Johnson. My husband was an express guard. One of the men Ben Whitlow killed."

After that, she seemed to think she'd said plenty. The Widow Johnson bustled a bit as she showed Tree a ground-level room in the rear that was neat as a pin and had starched curtains and a wider-than-average bed. There was a lone chiffonier and a cloudy mirror. Good enough. "If you'll require meals, Mr. Tree—"

"I'd figured to eat in town. My hours ain't always regular."

"That'll be fine."

He stashed the traveling bag, paid for three days in advance, and told her he'd be stepping out for a late supper.

"Mr. Tree," she said, walking with him to the door. Her voice was fervent, more husky than before. "I been a Christian woman all my life. Kind words for all God's children were on my lips. I was one to turn the other cheek. But things been rough since my dear Hubert lost his life. Very rough. We only had a little money saved."

Tree just nodded.

"I'm proud to have you staying at my house, Mr. Tree. Powerful proud. I want you to hang that scum Ben Whitlow high, and with no thought of mercy. I aim to be foremost in the crowd at the gallows. I aim to cheer."

The coffee was cold. Good and strong, but cold. Tree set the white china mug on the cafe table beside his empty plate that a half hour ago had held steaming steak and potatoes. He forked the last chunk of apple cobbler into his mouth and decided not to trouble the old-bat waitress for any more of the chicory-laced brew tonight. Maybe he'd mosey over to a saloon instead, the Bijou, and have a tot of refreshing beer. A glance at the Waterbury told him it was well past nine.

A full day, mostly of travel, put behind him, another one shaped up for tomorrow. A hangman's first day of preparations in a town were always busy: gallows to inspect, the culprit's weights to take, the general careful look-over of equipment. And there were the usual post-travel refreshments; the bath, haircut, and barbershop shave. Best to turn in earlier than later. He pushed his chair back, stood up, and ambled to the front to pay. Pocketing his change, the hangman stepped through the door and stood silhouetted for a moment in yellow window light. He bent his head and touched a sulfur match to a quirly.

One of the men lounging in the inky dark at the side of Roy's Livery Stable murmured to the other, "That him?"

"Sure as hell," was the reply. "Zack 'Hanging'

Tree, no less. Th' sheriff blabbed the truth in the Silver Slipper."

"Damn!"

"Throw a kink in your plans?"

"A bit." Tree was already moving off in the direction of some of the larger saloons. The pair weren't interested in following; the time had come for talk. "And this Tree ain't your ordinary hangman?"

"Bet your last peso, he ain't. Gives a clean, quick drop every time. But that ain't your main concern, I reckon. It's th' other, right? What I mentioned about Tree's wanting to be sure the law's got the right man? If there's something fishy in the trial, bribed jurors, lying witnesses, he'll find it all out."

The voices rang hollowly in the puddled shadows. The taller, broader, dark form shoved off from the wall. "Tree'll do that? What's his game? Take money off the condemned jasper?"

"Nothin' like that. They say he cares about justice."

The big man kicked the ground. "Why him?"

"Feller as th' presiding judge sent for. Ain't your say-so, ain't th' sheriff's. Reckon the hangman's going to make trouble for you?"

"If he don't move fast on stringing up Whitlow, the minute Tree starts to sniff around . . ." The big man stood up tall and drew his finger across his throat. His companion saw the gesture despite the night. A pale sliver of moon had appeared from behind a cloud.

The runt chuckled. "Can I be in on it?"

"Maybe you'll be needed, maybe not."

"Aww . . ."

At the intersection of the main street with the railroad, Tree turned into the Bijou Saloon. The bat-wings swung, he tipped his hat back, and disappeared into the blaze of light and flood of noise.

Chapter Four

Tree woke early in the bright, clean room he'd rented at Mrs. Johnson's and lay a minute just staring at the pale pink flowered wallpaper. The soft, bug-free tick he'd spent the night on was a fine luxury, but he was in Red Bluff to do a job, and this was a day for preparations. He rose and rummaged in his traveling bag for clean long-handled underwear and socks, letting alone the pinioning straps and other hangman's paraphernalia, which he'd inspect later. His pants and shirt hung in the cubbyhole closet, and he dressed rapidly, stepping into his stovepipe black boots last.

Then he sat down on the bedstead again, reached, and pulled from beneath the pillow a small, blued revolver. He twirled the cylinder of the Hopkins and Allen Captain Jack Model .32

and checked the five loads. Then he ever so carefully inserted it in the supple goatskin holster sewn inside his right boot. Finally, the last thing before stepping out the door, he strapped on his big holstered Colt .44–40 with the six-inch barrel.

Armed doubly, with one weapon chosen for firepower, the other for concealment, he felt ready for anything.

Outside the sun shone brightly, if not yet warmly on his wide, black-clad shoulders. First he'd set the bath and shave, following with breakfast at the same reasonably priced eatery he'd tried last night.

Although the hanging trade was brisk and he earned good money, Tree had never acquired the taste for fancy dining. Steak and potatoes for supper, ham and eggs for breakfast when available, and jerky and parched corn on horseback between towns. Wholesome fare. Plain fare. His pa had enjoyed the same before his life was so ruthlessly cut short.

An hour later Tree emerged from the Deluxe Cafe with his belly full and his hair still faintly smelling of the macassar oil the barber had used. The clean underwear felt smooth on his fresh-scrubbed skin as he made his way across to the livery. The old Negro that he'd talked to before—he assumed the man's name was Roy—he found pitching hay into stalls so leisurely that he didn't even seem to be at work. Behind the black man stood another fellow, hulking in a suit, but wearing a hard and mean-eyed look.

The man's words came out rasping as he stabbed with his finger.

"So you got it straight now, Roy?"

"Yessir!"

"What'd I tell you?"

"That your wife, she'll be wanting your rig."

"What time?"

"After lunch."

"So have our matched team of dapple grays curried and hitched up."

"Hitched up. Yessir."

The large and ugly man turned on his heel and brushed past Tree into the street with not so much as a nod of howdy, nor a crack in his granite frown.

Brown Suit had looked familiar. He was older than the sheriff by at least a dozen years and heavier, but he still carried the same slack jaw, craggy brow, and nose—a broad Tennessee nose jutting between close-set eyes.

"Morning."

"Howdy, Mr. Tree," Roy said, tossing aside his fork. Time for a short rest.

"That other feller," said Tree. "The gent. He wouldn't be—?"

The heavy-lidded gaze fixed Tree. "Yeah, it'd be. Morgan Van Aalst, town banker. Rich as sin. Brother to the sheriff. Got him a young wife, Mr. Hangman."

Tree half smiled. "You know my business. Last night I told you just my name."

"Word gets around."

"That so?" Tree looked around for his horse. "You had any luck selling my horse."

"Ain't been time to have no luck." The black man spat. A drowned fly floated in tobacco juice. "You sure you want to get rid o' the black? He's a fine animal."

"I don't need a regular mount. Train's faster."

"Business is that good?"

"Has been."

"I'll get 'im sold. Take a day or two."

"Hurry it. I don't aim to stick around Red Bluff long."

"Do for poor Ben Whitlow, be on your way, hey?"

"That's right." Tree turned to go. Then asked, "You know Whitlow?"

The liveryman wagged his long, dark head. "Goin' to be hanged, ain't he?"

"The reason I'm here."

"All's I know is, Mr. Hangman, you're set to do in one good feller, you are, in old Caleb Whitlow's boy. Neither o' the two hates a nigger for th' color of his hide. Ain't too many in the territory like that."

Tree was walking out, but the liveryman wasn't through.

". . . not th' town law, nor th' poor-trash jurymen. For sure, not the snot-nosed judge down from th' capital. . . ."

Tree squinted in the bad light in the hall outside the jail cell, took the scale's reading, and committed it to memory. "A hundred and sixty-four pounds. All right, Whitlow. You can step off now."

Sheriff Van Aalst, behind his polished star, waved his long, drawn six-gun at the prisoner. "You heard the hangman! Move, boy!" Then, to Tree he offered, "Like I said, we could've made him strip to weigh. Still can."

"Clothes don't make difference enough to bother."

"One sixty-four pounds. How much drop'll it take to croak our Ben? The gallows a-building going to have the height?"

Ben Whitlow stood in his stockinged feet, staring past the other men, his face frozen as if carved of ice. The stubborn cleft chin was held high, like a man who was controlling real fear. Not a hard type, but a newcomer to outlaw ways. From what he'd heard and what he'd seen of the father, Ben Whitlow had been small fry all his life. Hardscrabble rancher in the hills. Few stock. Bad pasture. Most likely, the chance had come along to get his hands on some quick money.

Tree doubted Whitlow had been the one to plan the robbery. Blocking the tracks, blowing the train's big safe—that took know-how. Tree guessed that Ben's companions—the ones that got away with the cash—

Van Aalst interrupted the hangman's thoughts. "Confound it, what about my question? The gallows— "

"I'll answer it after the lockup. No need to talk in front of the prisoner."

"Coddling an owlhoot? Hell—"

The lawman clamped his mouth closed. A glare from Tree could usually shut off fool talk like a spigot.

For the next few minutes, Tree worked silently, efficiently, sizing up the condemned man: his flesh tone, his general stature. At last he stepped up close and said, "Whitlow, I got to touch your neck."

The young man's expression changed. Cold impassivity was replaced by agitation. The hands at Whitlow's sides trembled. "No!"

Van Aalst's Colt rose to head level, and the sheriff thumbed to full-out cock. The click sounded like a cannon shot. "Watch it, feller!"

Tree said softly, "Yeah. I got to feel the tendons under your jaw."

"No!"

"I figure the drop by cyphering weight and force. All culprits are different. I aim to save you from the pain."

Ben Whitlow's face was a mask of rage. "I can stand pain, mister. If I'm dead, it won't matter if my neck is stretched ugly. Not to me!"

The sheriff snarled. "Feller—"

"Screw you! Screw the whole bloodthirsty crew!"

"I'll come back another time," Tree said.

"Screw you, hangman! Sheriff, you want to shoot, shoot! What I got to lose?" Ben Whitlow hurled himself across the floor, fists doubled, and launched a punch at Tree. Tree stepped sidelong from the man's path, and Whitlow brushed by. Tree's knuckles met his gut hard. Whitlow's mug turned the color of putty, his limbs to mush. He sank to his knees, then fell over.

"Don't shoot, sheriff!"

"And rob you of your wages? Fear not, Tree." A hammy hand descended to the fallen prisoner's collar, and showing surprising strength, Cain Van Aalst yanked. Whitlow was lifted bodily and flung into the cell. Tree slammed the door with a ringing clang.

"There. That'll happen sometimes, Sheriff."

"When he comes 'round, I'll work him over. Have my deputies in with clubs. Oh, yeah, I got a couple. Half-timers, help make the saloon patrol, quiet down the drunks. But the pair are handy as hell with leaded whipstocks, too."

"I'd be obliged if you let the prisoner be. I got him judged just fine, neck and all. I make out the drop for Ben Whitlow's requirements as four feet, six inches."

From the floor of the cell came a bitter laugh. "A four-foot-six drop for to hang Ben Whitlow? When he never killed nobody, done no crime? Ha!"

Ignoring the remark, Tree gathered up his gear and tugged down his hat brim. "By the way, Sheriff, I seen your brother this morning. Quite a family resemblance. But not a sociable gent much, is he?"

"Morg the banker? Friendly? He's a skinflint!

44

What'd you expect?" Cain Van Aalst wiped sweaty palms on his pant legs and erupted with a "Hmph!" Then he added, "Uses his power to help his kin out, though." He winked. "How you reckon I got this job?"

Tree left Sheriff Cain Van Aalst in the clammy, cut-stone jailhouse to while away the rest of the morning shuffling dodgers or napping with his feet cocked up high on his desk. The hangman greatly doubted that the badge toter would be hustling about in actual law-enforcement chores. For sure, he was possum lazy as well as tarantula mean.

But at least Tree didn't wonder any longer how the flabby son of a bitch had become top law dog in the region.

The sun was straight overhead in the blue dome of high-country sky. Noon, maybe a little after. Passing the livery stable on his way up the street, Tree noticed the matched pair of grays coming out the door in gleaming harness, prancing out in a fast, high-stepping trot. The carriage that they drew, a bright red surrey with a fringe-decorated canopy, raised brown clouds of street dust from its spinning wheels. But the jauntiest sight of all was the driver, a woman in a feathered hat. Gold hair blew back in the wind from one of the loveliest sets of features Tree had ever had the pleasure to view. The bloom of youth was on her cheeks, and her eyes flashed energetic fire.

Maybe that energy was the key to her, what made Morgan Van Aalst's beautiful wife go driving alone. Yeah, that's who it had to be: Mrs. Van Aalst. The description he'd heard earlier fit the buggy she was driving.

It was true as hell that she was younger than her husband by a long shot. She snapped her whip and sped on past as Tree watched from the boardwalk. When she was gone he stepped into the street to cross the busy thoroughfare crowded with ranch wagons and hurrying riders.

Moving along the boardwalk in the direction of the depot, he found himself in front of the Bijou and held up his steps. His mouth was dry, and a beer would taste just fine about now. And he recalled from his visit here last night that the place offered a free lunch. He turned that way and picked up his pace, but before he'd quite made it to the welcoming bat-wings, a sharp hissing sound reached his ears. Tree stopped stone still, his eyes drawn to the alley along the building's slab-board side.

A man stood beckoning him from the shadows there—an old man, ramrod straight with jutting white chin whiskers. It was old Caleb Whitlow. He made the hissing noise again with his tight lips, gestured once more, then ducked behind the wall and out of sight.

There had been a different look about the old fellow today . . . sane, not crazy. Likely, the drinks had had a chance to wear off.

But Tree loosened his six-gun in its holster before he strode after the old-timer.

He couldn't muster a whole lot of trust for the father of the man he'd come to hang.

Chapter Five

It was more of a straight, narrow passage between structures than a true alley. Windowless, shadowed, it smelled of garbage and dog shit, Tree noted fleetingly as he entered it to follow the white-bearded man. Old Caleb Whitlow was standing silhouetted against shafted sun's brightness behind him, and as the hangman approached cautiously, he spoke. "I'm glad you're willing to palaver private thisaway, Mr. Zachariah Tree. I don't much care to have the sheriff see us together."

Tree stopped a pace or two short of the speaker. The old man's features seemed to show an inner pain now, when viewed at close range. It might have been a miserable headache, the aftermath of a binge, but then it could be something else. Like cold fear of what was happening to his only son. "And what difference might it make, Whitlow, if the law does know we're having us a talk? Ain't against any law I've heard tell of. I'd have reckoned you'd be scared of me, after the trick you pulled last night."

"Trying to stick you with my toad-stabber? Damn stupid, I'll allow. Goddamn snakehead whiskey I been taking to lately. Lost my head."

"You had the wits to light out when I was looking the other way."

The old man's face, already grim, turned grimmer. "My boy was being beat up in his cell. I lit a shuck so's to stay free to help him later. Which brings us to now."

Tree scratched his chin. "That's what you want to jaw with me about, old man? I'm the hangman come to town to send off Ben Whitlow on the gallows. And I ain't ever yet failed to see my culprit dead with his neck stretched. I don't mean to start now."

"That's my goddamn point!" A strange look had come over Caleb Whitlow. The seams in his weather-beaten face deepened, and his eyes glazed over. "I tried talking with everybody hereabouts that's got to do with law," he told Tree. "The judge, when I spoke up at Ben's trial. Afterward the badge toter Cain Van Aalst. None of them will believe me when I say the boy's innocent!"

"Innocent?"

"Bet your boots!"

"The law says he's guilty, old-timer. When in the course of a crime, men get killed—"

"Then, who 'zactly pulled the triggers don't signify. Yeah, that's what was said at the trial." The old man nodded.

"Ben's a clean-cut-appearing young feller," Tree acknowledged. "But the robbers he was with when they hit that train—"

"Shit!"

"Old man, there's three express guards dead."

"Mr. Zachariah Tree, you got the face of a fair man, not one to go off half-cocked, even your trade being what it is. Y'see, Red Bluff's a railroader's town, Boyle's a railroad man, and all the jury at Ben's trial was all railroaders. Being from outside, maybe you can see the boy didn't get a fair shake. You be the only chance left anymore for my Ben. You will try, won't you, to find out the why of Boyle's story? I ain't a begging feller, Mr. Tree, b-but . . . please?"

"Boyle's still around town?"

"He is."

It was something to think on for a spell, anyhow. "I ain't going to make no promises, Whitlow. I wouldn't get my hopes up. The execution, it's set for the day after tomorrow. I got things to see to and—"

"You do aim to help! I can read it in you, by God!"

Tree fixed him with a frowning stare. "Fair is all I am, not charitable. My job's justice, and justice for them as done wrong, it's hard as hell."

The station agent didn't look up, and Tree could see why.

In front of the man with the green suspenders and eyeshade, the telegraph key was rattling fit to bust. The hangman took a few minutes to peer around the interior of the busy depot. An enormous potbelly stove was surrounded by ranked oak benches for the waiting passengers, and a large framed sheet of slate nearly filled a wall. On the slate were chalked the train schedules, with expected times and days of arrivals and departures neatly lettered in columns with chalk.

The telegraph stopped making its racket, and the agent jotted some notes on a pad in the center of his desk. Then he turned his head up and asked, "You want to buy a ticket, mister? First I got to know your direction; west or east."

"What I stopped by for is information," Tree replied. "I'm told Justin Boyle is working out of here these days. He's the one I got to talk to."

"Say, ain't you the hangman, Tree?" The agent had let his focused specs slide down his nose.

"I been knowed to answer to the handle."

"Well, I can tell you this much. Yeah, Boyle's been working out of Red Bluff, though his regular office is in Cheyenne. Took hisself over that desk in the corner. As you can see, he ain't in now. Figure him to be in on tonight's six-fifteen."

"Five hours?"

"More or less."

"I'll be back," Tree assured the man.

"Mr. Tree?"

"Yeah?"

"As a railroad employee, I'm right proud to meet you. Glad you come, glad you'll hang that scum, Ben Whitlow, high. Them outlaws need the lesson."

Tree touched his black hat's brim, smiled slightly, and left.

As he approached the jail, heading up the street, he saw the labor on the scaffold rolling merrily along. No fewer than three carpenters armed with hammers and saws were scrambling on the structure. A fourth was unloading raw lumber from a wagon box.

"Yo, Mr. Tree!"

"Howdy." He hoped the spokesman could hear over the pounding.

"How do you think she's shaping up?"

"Well, since you ask . . ." Tree broke off his words and hauled himself up the partially constructed steps to the platform; still-rough boards with plenty of spaces yet to be filled in. The framework where the trapdoor would go was complete, however; square, with the open area allowing clear looks down at street dust.

"Well, the floor appears to be high enough."

"A good and solid six and a half feet up off the ground we're a-standing!" the carpenters' foreman boasted. "Had the crowd in mind when we hammered her together!"

Tree snorted. "There's more important concerns than folks that admire the air dance. Mainly, it's the length of the drop so's the culprit dies sure and quick-like." His sharp and raking gaze took in everything the men with tools were doing, from planning boards propped on sawhorses to pounding huge, square, hand-forged nails. The semi-completed "crossbeam on uprights" appeared sturdy, an important consideration. But there was something Tree didn't like one tiny bit. "Son of a bitch! This ain't going to do!"

The chief hammer-and-saw man was crest-fallen. "Er, what do you mean?"

"I don't guess the trap itself is built yet?"

"The fellers been puttin' in plenty long hours, but—"

"It ain't, then? That's good. Won't need to do it all over. Look here. The size of the space the culprit will drop through; what is it, maybe two feet by two? Not big enough. There can be twitching or lurching just at the second that the lever gets yanked, and that can mean a queer drop. I've seen men's chins smashed to smithereens underneath their dying hoods. Noses sheered off as if axed."

"Who the hell cares?"

"Nearby townsfolk that get splashed with blood. And tell me this: you ever met an undertaker who's easy to deal with?"

The foreman's voice had turned humble. "Make the door wider?"

A grim hangman nodded. "And the best quality factory hinges, if you please. Hinges are important—damned important. Savvy?"

And the hangman leaped from scaffold to the street, landing cat footed and lofting powdered dust. "Go on ahead, fellers. Carry right on!" The hangman left the work area behind with long, rapid strides and headed for Mrs. Johnson's rooming house. If Ben Whitlow's hanging was going off as planned, he had an afternoon's toil ahead preparing his rope and prisoner harness.

An acetylene lamp slung from a ceiling hook lit the depot with a dazzling white glare. All the desks, chairs, and cabinets squeezed into the office end behind he tickets grille were set off in harsh relief. Railroad light, Tree told himself as he was let past the raised plate of counter by the dispatcher. Modern inventions. Now we can all go blind from this one. He strolled to the corner desk, sizing up the man there as he went. Early thirties. Freshly shaven despite the hour, dressed in shirtsleeves and a leather vest. He had a full head of hair, the color of burnished pewter.

"Zachariah Tree?" The gray-haired man rose and extended his hand. "Melvin mentioned you'd been by. Said you'd be back. Glad to oblige you, sir."

"Boyle," Tree said, "I'd be much obliged if you could give me some background on—"

"The Whitlow case. Yes, I can see your want.

You have the reputation, sir, of being careful in your trade."

Tree stood in silence. Boyle began, "Please pull a chair up and sit down."

He'd swept a sheaf of papers from the desk and now brought out a box. He thumbed up the tin lid. "Cigar?"

Tree shook his head. "But go on ahead." Boyle did so, and soon the corner reeked with expensive smoke.

"Boyle, I'll get right to it. Your court testimony's what condemned Whitlow."

Boyle puffed his stogie. "Fact, I admit."

"I heard you were called in pretty quick, Boyle, when the local law didn't make a catch right off."

Boyle ran his bony, strong fingers through his gray hair, wrinkled his brows, and glanced at the Regulator clock by which the trains ran. There was an eastbound train pulling in now with a series of chuffs, belches, and whining bleats of its whistle. The railroad cop waited a minute for the earsplitting noise outside to settle down. Then he spoke in an assured, calm voice, looking Tree square in the eyes.

"You have it right, Tree. I was called in soon—the very first day, in fact, that I could reach this place, making connections from Salt Lake City. When I got in, I found no one to update me—Sheriff Van Aalst was out combing with a posse. I commandeered an engine to get out to the site; it's just about five miles from Red Bluff. A place where the engines have to make a long upgrade pull. At the top of the cut was where the bandits blocked the track with ties. An expert job. I've seen few set up so clever."

"At this point you knew mainly that there was five outlaws, ten thousand dollars missing, and three guards dead."

"What came over the wires. Oh, and I'd been advised by my superior on the U. P. company police that the sheriff in these parts is a brutal clown who got to be law through influence. That's why I was on my own."

A crew of punchers just off the train were rowdily crossing the platform. Tree ignored the distraction. "Did you take up the chase then?"

"There was no time to lose. That's why I rode alone on the horse I brought in a stock car. I reasoned that since the sheriff and the townsmen he'd deputized were doing the job, I'd try something different and ride the notch up toward the divide. To make the story short, I got lucky. In soft sand beside a stream I picked up the tracks made by a slew of horses. Later there turned out to be five, when the gang split up."

"How'd you happen to pick Ben Whitlow to track?"

The railroad detective shrugged as he stubbed out his cigar. "I didn't pick Whitlow. I made a random choice from the five trails that led away from the stream. As it happened, after a long and winding ride through rough mountain country, I found myself overlooking a ranch. The ranch was Whitlow's, and a horse in the corral had a badly cracked shoe. It was the animal I'd been following."

"I see." What Tree didn't see quite so easily was how a jury was made to buy this evidence. The raiders of the train wore bandannas over their faces. Apparently the cracked-shoe horse's track wasn't seen at the scene. "After you brought in Ben Whitlow, did the sheriff trace back the trail you found?" Tree closely watched the pewter-haired man's eyes.

"As fortune would have it, that night a rain washed out all sign." Boyle held his hands out, palms out. "And if your next question deals with loot, no, it wasn't found."

"Outlaws took it?"

"Seems like it."

"Now it's all over, so why are you still in town? Ain't your regular base the division yards in Cheyenne?"

Boyle's expression changed.

"See here, Tree! I'm not carrying on some personal feud against Ben Whitlow."

Tree's sharp instinct told him to be going. He started to push back his chair and rise.

"I'm interested in the case, is all. I tracked the murderer and I mean to see him swing for his crimes. No, I'm not forgetting Hubert Johnson and the other murdered guards."

Zachariah Tree wondered about Boyle's eyesight, writing up reports by railroad light. It was brighter in the depot than ever. Objects assumed a silver sheen. "No, I reckon I can see your point," Tree said, heading for the door. "I'm a bulldog myself on things that catch my attention."

Two forms hunkered in the night's puddled shadows at the base of the big cottonwoods. From here they could see Tree's lit window in the rooming house with ease. Ann Johnson's curtains were lace, transparent with the lamp behind them. The silhouette moving from the washstand to the closet and back was the hangman, no mistake. And by the look of things, he'd soon be climbing into bed.

"See him?" the larger of the two men hissed. It was a stage whisper that grated the other's eardrums.

"Sure, asshole. Ain't I got eyes the same as you? Better'n your'n? Not even squinty and crossed?"

"Huh?"

"Yeah, it's 'Hanging' Tree in th' bedroom, right as rain."

"Now's the time to pick him off?" The figure shoved back its slouch hat.

"No, now *ain't* th' time! Didn't the boss say to watch tonight? Follow where he went, see who he talked to?"

"Be spies."

"Lookit! He's a-blowing out th' coal-oil lamp."

"Our chance?"

"To spy some more. 'Tain't midnight yet.

Midnight comes, th' boss, he'll sneak by. Decide what we're to do next."

"If he says to, hitting Tree's easy as hell. See the bedstead through the window? Blast the son of a bitch!"

"*If'n* th' boss says to."

"Yeah—if'n."

Chapter Six

Tree stirred fitfully and came awake in the room's still darkness, lit faintly by moonshine. Outside a screech owl was making its night calls. He rolled over in the bed and moved the pocket pistol from under his ribs to be more comfortable. Now the trick was to get back to sleep. But there were things on his mind, and he found it wasn't so easy. Involuntarily, his brain was ticking off points in the Whitlow case.

This was despite the fact that his profession was hangman, not investigator or redeemer of the condemned's lost causes. But, damn it, if he hated anything he saw in life, injustice was one of them.

The other was to see rightly convicted murderers and other villains slip from justice's grasp.

Now his thoughts were drifting back, back to the days down in south Texas before he'd entered the hanging trade.

He could see himself riding back to Vermilion after a visit to pretty Coralita Clive's pa's ranch. He was greeted by the sight of his own pa, Aaron, for whom he'd worked—facedown on the ground out in the rear of the jail. Back shot. Dead. As deputy, Zack Tree knew the town troublemakers, knew who had a grudge. There was a no-good who'd been locked up for a drunk rampage weeks before. A quick check at Josh Pingree's room revealed the jasper had left in haste.

Only after a furious pursuit and gun battle did Deputy Zack Tree bring in his father's killer. The country around and about were outraged at the crime. A swift trial, and Josh Pingree was found guilty and sentenced to hang.

The hangman was the blacksmith, strong of arm, but an amateur with a noose. The smith had dallied the rope around the saddle horn of the mount he straddled and pulled Josh Pingree up to a branch of the selected live oak. There was a lot of kicking and facial distortion as the townsfolk watched Josh strangle. Pronounced dead, the confessed murderer was cut down and laid in a pine coffin, taken charge of by the undertaker.

An hour later, the "corpse" vanished from the undertaker's premises. One of the hearse horses had been stolen, black plume and all. The smith was sorry about the bungled hanging that had left the victim alive and able to escape.

Josh Pingree was never chased down. Zachariah Tree spent a full year on the hunt, but the trail petered out.

Tree ended up in Waco, the Longhorn Saloon, with a mescal bottle in front of him on a scarred deal table, wondering why in the hell such things could happen. His father's killer got off free because of a bungled execution. A man near sixty, wearing a white goatee, a paunch, and a rumpled Prince Albert coat, wandered over on that hot, quiet afternoon. "I'm Orion Q. Partridge," the newcomer announced, throwing his bulk into a chair. "Mayhap you've heard of me. I've been hearin' around town some about the son of my old friend Aaron."

"Partridge, the hanging judge?" Tree remembered saying.

"The same. How'd you like to come work for me?"

Old Judge Partridge "apprenticed" young Tree under the best hangmen in all Texas, and the parts of the West. The lessons took and took well. Not much later, the former deputy was as good as his teachers.

Partridge retired from the bench two years later, and Zachariah Tree took his new profession traveling. And as the "Hanging Judge of Waco" had prophesied, now his name was known most places he went.

He was drowsy again, but another noise reached him from outside. It sounded like the crackling of underbrush. He got up and padded to the window. A quick scan about turned up nothing. Most likely the noise had been a scavenging cur, he thought. Shrugging, he went back to bed. That's just when whatever was out there chose to move again.

"Damn," Zach Tree grunted, pulling on his pants and stamping into his boots with long practice in getting quickly dressed. Inside ten seconds he was buckling on his gun belt, stepping silently through the house and slipping out the door. He didn't make directly for the cottonwood, although it was in the darkness under it where the trouble lay. He circled wide in a crouching run, Colt in hand.

Before he'd reached the concealment of the neighbor's fence, a man's shadowy form broke and fled. Tree took off after him, but the jasper was wiry and fast afoot. He dodged among the dark dwellings. A cat, somebody's pet, dashed past in the hangman's path, but he sidestepped and plunged on. Ahead was a shallow gully, and Tree was running downhill, keeping his quarry in view by moonlight, but not closing the distance. The small man was more determined to get away than ever. He jumped the stump of a fallen pine and rushed on.

They were at the town's edge now, and Tree heard running water. Among low willow saplings, pursued and pursuer plowed. Whipping branches slapped and stung Tree's skin. Then his boots were sucked by streamside mud. He held his big six-gun in front of him.

He nearly stumbled over the dark, huddled form that, by its shape, had to be a man. "Ah, there you are," Tree snapped, pointing the .45. "Now, why were you watching outside the window to my room?"

Silence.

"Talk, you bastard, else I'll—" But the rest of the threat was never uttered. A harsh grunt came from behind as the downed man's pard stepped from cover and swung a clubbed, twisted limb. Brittle wood slammed the back of the hangman's skull. Zach Tree collapsed.

"Kill him right here?" The voice echoed as though down in a foggy canyon. Tree attempted to rise, but couldn't.

"Can't 'thout the boss's order. We'd best clear out."

Tree heard departing footsteps and fought off dizzy feelings and pain until he felt a mite better. After a long while he was able to stand, albeit unsteadily.

"Damn bastards! But at least they left me my gun." He retrieved the weapon he saw glinting in the dewy grass.

"Enough headaches in this town. Now I found me another one." He hiked back to the rooming house.

Ann Johnson, widow, was plying her feather duster in her rooming house's parlor when the knock came at the front door. She pulled her apron straight and patted her bunned hair hurriedly in front of the hall mirror before answering. When she swung the door wide, there on the porch the large man stood, pink faced and important-looking in a suit of worsted. She recognized him immediately. Any resident of Red Bluff would have.

"Why, Mr. Morgan Van Aalst!"

"It's Miz Johnson, ain't it? Yeah, Miz Johnson, it's me. I'm told down at the bank this is where the hangman's staying whilst he's in town. Zachariah Tree, come to string up the Whitlow boy. That true, ma'am?"

She looked as puzzled as she felt. "Yes, it's quite true." To her, bankers mostly meant foreclosures. Hers had been a hard-luck family all their lives.

"Well, can I see Tree? Go tell him I'm here."

"Well, I'd like to but . . ."

"But he ain't up yet? It's early in the morning, I'll grant." Van Aalst peered past the woman fiercely.

"No, that's not it. I mean, it's early in the morning, all right, not yet nine. But what I mean to say is, he's not in bed."

"Woman, do you know who I am? That you're keeping me waiting?" He tried to squeeze his powerful form past the woman and across the threshold. "Where is he?"

"Not here."

"Woman! But you said—"

"Gone out! Mr. Tree, he's done gone out! 'Thout breakfast, 'thout taking time to shave. Hurried-like, you know?"

65

"Ahem." Now the man attempted dignity. "Ahem. Well . . . Yeah." He jammed the hat back on that he'd swept off, and cleared his throat a final time. "Then, I'll leave a message with you, Mrs. Johnson. Tell Mr. Tree he's invited to my house. Mrs. Van Aalst and myself, we're having leading citizens over tonight. Tomorrow's hanging day, and we want to meet the man. We're assuming, all of us, that once his job is through, he'll be leaving directly. Such a busy man. Goes from one hanging to the next by train."

She gawked at Morgan Van Aalst. "I'll tell him about your party."

"It's tonight, remember."

"Tonight."

She watched Van Aalst make his way back up the path to where his surrey waited. The very same one the stuck-up wife always drove about in. Silk dresses. Hats with paper flowers.

And poor Ann Johnson had been forced to sell her wedding ring to eat. She grimaced as she quietly shut her weathered front door.

Tree reined in the black gelding on the ridge overlooking the small ranch headquarters. It was much as he'd pictured it, knowing the Whitlows, father and son. The place was situated in a saucered depression surrounded by cut-up land: canyons, buttes, dry creek beds. The taller mountains reared to the north. The mere few alders and beech signaled a short water supply.

The buildings—a barn, two sheds, a half-log, half-stone main house—appeared in as good order as could be done without much money.

Tree winced. Of course, that was supposed to be the motive for the crime for which Ben Whitlow had been sentenced to hang: money to improve this spread.

He'd surprised Roy the liveryman and taken out the black this day to view the place. He wasn't one to ignore an appeal such as old Caleb Whitlow's. Especially now, since the run-in with those spying jaspers.

Caleb had declared positively that Ben was with him at the Double W on the night of the twenty-eighth, the night of the U. P. holdup. Courts tended to discount testimony sworn by close kin of defendants. He, Zachariah Tree, could choose to follow a hunch.

A few horses—common quarter-horse plugs—stood about the pole corral; skinny cattle cropped grass in the pasture. Other than these, Tree saw no sign of life. Gigging the black gelding down the slope, he cast about with his eyes, but the yard simply baked in the quiet sunshine. "Hello, the house," Tree called. No answer.

He stepped from leather and left the black untethered as he circulated from building to building. Beside a row of stacked stovewood he paused to mop his face.

Suddenly, a catapulting form raced across the

flat, swinging a grain shovel at Tree. Zachariah Tree dodged just in time and dipped beneath the intended blow. But then he felt the sting of a glancing hit to the shoulder as the stranger used his fist.

"What the hell—?"

"Take this, bastard!" Another swing, this time a looping roundhouse, but he missed. The shovel slipped from the man's grasp and lay harmlessly in the dirt. Recovering from his surprise, Tree stepped forward, his own hands clenched and clubbed. Staring hard at the jasper who'd jumped him, Zach Tree, never having seen the face before, set out to alter it. The hangman leveled a jab that connected with the man's nose and started it bleeding. Then his knuckles raked the stubbled cheek and sent the stranger sprawling.

On the ground, before he could squirm away from reach, the man felt Zachariah Tree's powerful grip lifting him by his shirt front.

"What say, feller? Call it quits?"

"Y-yeah! Shit, yeah!"

Tree released the jasper and let him flop on the ground like an emptied flour sack. Still angry, though defeated, the man shook his head as if to clear it. Lank, greasy hair flopped across a low, smooth forehead. The man managed to appear old and yet fairly young at the very same time. It was a look Tree had seen occasionally in feeble-minded folks. But at least this one wasn't giving him any more trouble.

"What you jump me for, man? You must have

seen or heard me ride up and call. You work for Caleb?"

"Caleb?"

"You know Caleb? Old geezer with the cue-ball dome, stained beard? Runs the Double W?"

"Yeah, sure. Caleb," he said with a vacant grin. "Buster knows Caleb."

"You're Buster?"

"Y-yeah."

Tree puzzled for about two seconds over how to handle this turn of developments, then decided to forge ahead with questions, the same as if he'd found old Whitlow at home. It occurred to him that Buster could be Whitlow kin.

"Buster," Tree said carefully, "you live on the spread, do you?"

A shake of the head.

"But hereabouts? Not far? Are you Whitlow kin?"

Too many queries at one time, the bewildered stare told Tree. He asked again. "You don't live here, but you come here." Buster nodded. "That's good. You seen Ben lately? No? Do you recollect how long it's been?"

Now the half-wit sat propped against the woodpile and seemed less fuddled. "Ain't seen Ben," he declared, "since the creek-flood rain. And me here every night playing checkers. Win matchsticks off Caleb. Plenty of matchsticks."

Interesting. "Ben was here the night of the big rain. And the day and the night before. Does Ben play checkers, too, Buster?"

A pause. A scratch of the stomach. A scratch

of the rump inside patched pants. Then he blurted, "Ben, he plays checkers, damn good checkers. But Ben, he weren't t'home night afore th' big rain."

"Weren't?"

"Nossir!"

"Buster, are you sure? Old Caleb, he's gone and told me Ben was right here to home on the Double W that night. That's when a train was held up down the mountain. That's the night before the big rain that we been jawing about."

"Buster can remember! Can't read nor cipher, but he can play checkers and remember stuff! And Buster remembers Ben gone off to—"

As Tree peered into stammering Buster's face, it suddenly caved inward, the eyes popping like exploding grapes. The hulking body jumped and jerked, twisting. Tree saw the fountaining bullet hole at the half-wit's temple, and from the ridge beyond, he made out the pale puff of rifle's smoke. The report at this distance was a flat *crack*, echoing. The hangman sidelonged just in time; another shot followed the first, the slug whistling near his ear. He grabbed at the Colt in his holster, dove for cover, but that was when the deep *boom* went off behind some scrub piñons up the opposite slope. The sound of a long Sharps's .50! The slug ripped the heel from his right boot. Fierce pain lanced through his leg.

He was yards from his horse, hunkered behind Buster's bloodied corpse. And the bushwhackers began laying down a shower of steady fire from outside six-gun range.

70

Chapter Seven

The 550-grain rifle slug slammed a flat rock close to Zachariah Tree's leg, and glanced and careened away crazily to punch through the lean-to. An instant later, another bullet and yet a third plowed sod and buried themselves in the grotesquely sprawled corpse of Buster. If he was going to stay alive, Tree needed cover fast. He threw a shot from his Colt despite the range and raked his glance around the sparse side yard of the Double W Ranch headquarters.

The woodpile was at his back. A dozen yards off to his left leaned a small, square outhouse. The main house was even farther, and the barn loomed beyond that. As two more rounds nearly found him, one tugging his sleeve, he made up his mind, rolled from his proximity to the dead man, got to his feet, and sprinted toward a shallow gully. Within the gully, he could see, it was dense with claw-branched serviceberry.

With a spring and a dive, the hangman plunged into the thicket. Branches raked his hands and his face. He hobbled quickly on the boot without a heel. Shots from the ridges continued to pour, but thus far, at least, Tree remained unhit and unhurt.

Damned lucky.

The minute he sensed himself screened from the ambushers up top, he ceased running and dropped to the ground. He circled back to the shrubbery's ragged edge, crawling, his six-gun out and ready. He peered between twigs and leaves teased by the ceaseless wind, but saw no one. The ambushers weren't stirring.

Or perhaps they were already on the way down by hidden routes. They had to have spotted where he'd scrambled to hole up. They'd leave their snipers' posts if it meant flushing him.

Silent waiting spun out; the warm sun beat on Tree's hunched-down back. Gnats swarmed the thicket and descended on him relentlessly. The stinging pain in his ankle and foot made him unsure of his ability to run, especially with a busted heel on his boot. His strong hunch told him to play the cards as they'd been dealt, not let impatience trick him.

He made a few seconds go by easily by reloading, thumbing fresh shells into the Colt's chambers with practiced skill. He spun the well-oiled cylinder of his weapon, then reached to loosen the Captain Jack pistol inside his boot top. He shifted position to ease the tension in his limbs and squinted under his Stetson's brim.

All of a sudden, one attacker came charging across the flat! At the same moment, renewed repeater fire from the basin's rimrock peppered the dig-in.

Ignoring the whining slugs, Tree cocked and triggered, laying down his own wall of flying lead for the charging man to eat. Stumpy legs pumping over the short-grassed flat, the man zigzagged to avoid Tree's bullets.

One of the hangman's bullets plugged his hat, and it kited away. He kept on coming. Running straight up to the gully's tip, he threw the big Sharps single-shot to his shoulder and sighted down the glittering barrel. Tree saw the massive hammer at full cock. He hiked on his elbows and brought the Colt to bear.

The exploding roar of the .50 drowned out the flat report of the fanned .45. The men had both fired their weapons at the precise same instant. Tree felt a surge of heat flush his face. No pain, though. Tree had rolled as he'd triggered. Flat on his back, he was looking upward. A squat form shadowed out the sky.

"Aaaiiee!" The howl was beastlike; pure, seething agony. Tree's attacker's mouth pulsed and wrapped around the piercing cry. The man fell to his knees and flung his head back. Blood and green bile sprang brightly to soak the shirt below the short man's stomach. "Gutshot! I'm gutshot!" The rifle dropped from the quaking hands which quickly flew to the wound. Instantly the hands were bloodied. Shortly pitched to the earth. He kicked, he bucked, then sagged and lay spasming, twitching horribly for another few seconds. Then the bulging eyes rolled back. The man was still.

Tree climbed to his feet, the six-gun filling his big right fist, turned his back on the dead fellow, and struggled up the brush-choked gully. Now that the odds had evened gun-wise, he sought to take the battle to the sniper up top. He found the going rough on his sore ankle, but he plowed on doggedly. When he was in the clear, he saw straight ahead the fan-shaped shale slope.

From the crest, he just might find himself above the sniper. Or he could meet him face to face.

Tree sucked in his breath and rubbed his troublesome leg through the leather of his boot. Gripping his Colt butt tightly, he started up. The hangman's boot soles scraped and slid with every attempted step. Rain had washed away all soil from the trail, leaving nothing but round, loose gravel. He soon gave up watching where he put his feet, and let the stones roll where they would.

A jackrabbit scuttled from his path. Tree wiped sweat from his brow with his sleeve and kept on climbing.

Not far from the jagged rampart, the hangman gritted his teeth. Once there, he'd prove his Colt quicker than any Winchester. And his expert close-range marksmanship could determine the skirmish winner.

He reached the summit without attracting another shot. He stepped quickly over and into a small stand of Norway spruce, but Tree detected no sign of activity. Birds were quiet; no animals stirred. Someone was close by. The hairs at Tree's nape seemed to prickle and jump. It was a sixth sense he'd learned to trust.

He edged slowly, slowly from the protection of an enormous rock pillar.

The next second, hot lead slapped the rock face and sang away in a screaming ricochet. A pale, sheared scar gleamed only inches from Tree's drawn face.

The hangman crouched, wedged into a man-sized niche in the granite wall, six-gun cocked, unmoving, but straining to listen. The silence was as deafening as the earlier volleys of shots. The sun broiled down. Nothing moved. It occurred to Tree that things could be worse. All he had to do was wait.

The musical tingle of a spur sounded, and Tree leaped from his place of hiding, Colt blazing. He fired from the hip, but with expertly judged aim. The man in front of him spun to look, started to raise his Winchester, then gasped to find the carbine blown from his hands. The man spun and broke into a run. Tree's next shot grazed his pumping arm. He yelped, then vanished behind a verticle wall. Tree plunged in pursuit of the fleeing bushwhacker, but slipped, due to his absent bootheel.

There was plenty of noise in the air now. Saddle leather creaked as a hurt man struggled to mount. Then a harsh "Giddap!" A ragged thrumming of hooves. Damn! And if the son of a bitch were getting away . . .

The man had gotten away, Tree realized grimly. He heaved erect and followed as quickly as he could around the trail's next bend. The first object to catch his eye was a horse, the horse of the dead bushwhacker, saddled and hobbled.

Tree mounted and rode the shagged dun around the long way and came into the yard from the other end. Without delay, he loaded the two corpses, Buster's and the short man's.

It was a far piece to town, and he had other matters aplenty to tend to this afternoon. . . .

Cain Van Aalst wasn't in the jail office when Tree trudged in, but a deputy was. This badge packer looked to be a drinking pard of the chief law dog. The same age, approximately, the same slack expression. Certainly the same tiny, cruel eyes. The man slouched in the chair behind the desk and peered up grudgingly. "Sheriff's gone to supper, Hangin' Tree. Left me in charge. Said to watch the prisoner, keep out visitors."

"You got a name?"

"It's Ike. Ike McGraw."

Tree sighed. "Two things, McGraw." He

spoke to him as if to a child. "One is, I got me a handle, too, that I like. And that's Zachariah Tree. 'Hanging' is what I do, not who I am. And second, seeing why I'm in town, I ain't Ben Whitlow's visitor. I'll see him as I choose, and I choose right now."

"I dunno—"

"I do know this. Outside at the hitch rail there's a tired dun bronc. It's tired on account of dead men—two—tied on its back. One corpse I call Buster; that's what he called himself. The other's a stranger to me."

"What—"

"The stranger killed Buster and tried to shoot me; him and a pard. I killed this one, his pard lit out. Now, McGraw, who's in charge, what you going to do about it?" Tree slapped the desk, grinned.

"Christ! I'll go find Cain!"

"And I'll see to the prisoner while you're out. Good luck."

After McGraw snatched up the keys and stalked out, Tree bent wearily, rubbed his sore ankle, and adjusted his boot. Once he got the shot-off heel fixed, he'd be well nigh fixed, he knew. And he presumed the town of Red Bluff had a shoemaker. Now for the prisoner. Tree limped stiffly toward the lockup, whistling between his teeth.

No sense letting on that things had gotten puzzling as hell. Not if he aimed to persuade Ben Whitlow to provide him some answers.

The condemned man lay on the flat, hard

board cot that the county provided jail inmates. He had to be uncomfortable, even though his face retained the sullen stare. Tree stood and peered at Whitlow between the floor-to-ceiling bars. Ben Whitlow looked back, frowning, and didn't speak at first. But then the chiseled jaw dropped and the words started coming out a mile a minute. "What the devil you doing back here again, hangman? Ain't you going to see enough of me in the morning? That is when you're fixed to march me to the scaffold, I understand. Then you and this whole god-damned pitiful town can reckon you got the better of me. Of a feller who's been easy pickings!"

"Why you tell me that, Whitlow? The part about being easy?"

He sneered. "Well, I didn't put up much fight when that railroad dick polecat whipped out handcuffs and threw them on me. I didn't know yet what he was charging me with. And later he and the others made short work of me at the trial."

"Your trial?"

"Their trial. It had no part of me 'cept I was made to be there. I weren't guilty. Not of robbery. Not of murder. Don't even know no thieving, killing owlhoots."

Tree fished out the makings. "Justin Boyle thinks you do."

"Justin Boyle's an asshole."

Tree shook Union Leader carefully into the piece of rolling paper he thumbed. He tugged the sack drawstring with his teeth and finished building the quirly. "Smoke, Whitlow?"

"I don't smoke."

"Got not cut plug for to offer."

"You figure I chaw? Huh!"

Tree bored him with his eyes. "What do you do for pleasure, then? Ever play checkers? With your paw? With a feller name of Buster?"

For the first time Ben Whitlow's face showed interest. The young man reared from the cot and approached on stockinged feet. "I overheard your meeting up with paw." A bitter chuckle. "You know Buster, too? Tree, why'd you come here today?"

"Palaver. Maybe you ain't guilty like they claim. Maybe the hanging can be put off. Maybe the real killers can be found. A lot of maybes, wouldn't you say? But if you want help, you got to help me some."

A sidelong look. "How?"

Tree was talking rapidly now, glancing over his shoulder. What he was saying wasn't Van Aalst's business, should the lawman walk back in here among the cells. "I rode out to your spread this morning, Whitlow. Aimed to talk to old Caleb another time. Met this Buster instead. Not too bright upstairs, maybe, but real interesting. Talked some on checkers and such."

A small grin formed on the prisoner's lips. "Buster works around the place. We cheer him up by playing his game."

"See if this cheers you. He said you weren't to home the night of the U. P. holdup. That means your paw lied. Means you could've been in on the express job. Unless—"

Whitlow furiously bit out, "Goddamn! Listen, fetch Buster here, Mr. Hangman! I'll pound the story out of the jughead! I'll—"

"Not so fast! Buster's dead, Ben. Old Caleb didn't turn up, so he's more than likely safe, but a bushwhacker shot Buster cold. Tried to nail my hide. You're wondering why I come? The ambush answers it. Somebody don't want me nosing around."

"Buster dead? Jesus!"

"I brought one ambusher back, ready to plant in boot hill. The other hightailed. Since those two opened fire from the far ridge, they could only guess at what Buster was telling me. Likely, they figured Buster said things that'd clear you. He didn't, but now I'm left plumb curious."

"Buster dead . . . I'll be goddamned!"

"Where are you the night of the robbery? Buster was simple minded, but I don't believe that he was wrong about who played checkers when. I asked you before what you did for pleasure, and I recall you turned the question aside. Now I'll put it another way, Ben Whitlow. Ain't it true you got you a woman?"

Suddenly a fire burned in the condemned man's eyes. Tree had seen the rage the day before, when Ben Whitlow had bristled violently in asserting his innocence. Now, when Whitlow was hot, Tree decided to be mountain-spring cool. He calmly placed in his mouth the quirly he'd rolled, and thumbed alight a lucifer. "Well?"

As the hangman touched the small flame to stoke his smoke, Ben Whitlow steamed inside. The working lips told it, as did the prisoner's strained neck tendons. He was taut as a fiddle bow. Nearly a half-minute had passed when he thought it best to speak. Tree was mildly disappointed at what he said.

"What makes you ask, have I got a gal friend? Mr. Hangman, you got to be loco."

"You're the loco one, playing this way with your life."

"No woman!"

"Liar!" Tree's steely eyes were as hard as the jail bars. Now he locked the pair directly on the condemned man's and hissed out, "The only critter you might do what you're doing is a woman. You got to be protecting somebody. Somebody whose name would be mud if word got out they was with you. Sounds like a woman, and a married woman, I'd be willing to bet my hat. But she ain't worth it."

"Not worth risking my neck for, you mean."

"I mean *stretching* your neck. She's worthless, if she didn't come forward at your trial."

"Damn it, Tree," Ben Whitlow roared. "There's no woman, I say! Don't you mix in this thing!"

Tree raised his hand when he heard the door slam in the front office, and turned to see big Cain Van Aalst coming along the corridor. "Afternoon, Sheriff."

"Two dead men," the law dog grumbled. "Ike said you got surprised on the trail, hangman. True?"

"True enough." Tree considered briefly as he tossed the quirly down, stamped it out. "The one corpse was a waddie at the Whitlows' place, where all this happened. Like I told Deputy Ike, the bushwhacker I didn't ventilate managed to get away. Makes me think some."

"Be relieved when his hanging's over and done?"

Sheriff, I'm never easy if there's a chance I'd be doing in the wrong man. Sometimes juries make mistakes. I'd like a day to sniff around."

The sudden red cast of Van Aalst's face looked dangerous. "Hell, no, Tree! Whitlow strings tomorrow! The town committee is in on this; the circuit judge and all! They printed invitations are even passed out as of this morning!"

"I had me a close scrape today, Van Aalst. I'll make it clear like this: the hanging has been postponed. Now I'm heading for my rooming house."

"My brother and his missus's party, it's—"

"One of them execution-eve get-togethers, town bigwigs and such? Never cared for them." Tree stalked past the sheriff, and out through the office into the street. Outside, the late-day sun hung in a sky of brass.

The scent of fresh lumber and sawdust perfumed the air. Zachariah Tree was confronted by the looming new gallows. The structure was a six-foot-high platform—above that, twin uprights and a crossbeam. Fixed into the beam was a strong steel hook. It all appeared a trim job of construction.

"What you thinking, Mr. Hangman?" It was the same workman who'd spoken up before. "Fixed the trap just like you said to. In the morning we test it one last time. Then it's Ben Whitlow's turn!"

Tree nodded. "Make your test right careful." Then he moved off in the direction of a cobbler's shop he'd spotted.

Chapter Eight

"Dammit to hell, that light!" Morg Van Aalst blustered as if to blind a man, his cruel eyes pinched into a squint.

"Acetylene."

"Too damn bright!"

"Progress, Morg," the sheriff said, dropping his bulk into a chair. "Way of the future. Ain't that c'rect, Justin?"

Railroad Detective Boyle of the Union Pacific gestured, taking in the whole depot interior from door to ticket cage. He grinned. "All of it, friends. All of it."

"You're just used to them Frenchified lamps in that mansion of yours, Morg." Cain Van Aalst laughed.

"All right, Cain, why'd you call us three

together?" The banker, now seated, too, was fingering an enormous cigar.

"Well . . ."

"Out with it, Cain," Justin Boyle put in, smoothing his unnaturally metallic thatch with the flat of a hand.

"Yeah, I'd best come to the point. It's this. The hangman, Tree, he's gone and called off Whitlow's meeting with the noose. For tomorrow, anyhow. Walked into the jailhouse and just said it. Something 'bout, maybe the law caught us the wrong man."

Gone as suddenly as a high-plains thundershower were the pleasant expressions. Morgan Van Aalst's face reddened with anger. Boyle grimaced grimly and his eyes went to ice. "That purely don't sound good," snapped the railroad dick. "Fact is, it's plumb insulting. To the town, of course, where the trial jurors came from. But to you, too, Cain. And me."

"Mostly you. You brung Ben Whitlow in."

"And proud to say so!"

The banker drew on his cigar thoughtfully. "Makes sense now, Tree's not showing at the house."

"Damn it, Morg! What's important here?" Seeing the others' bad reaction, the sheriff was on his feet. "Not your tea party!"

"Not only that, no. There's them invites, and the town committee . . ."

"The committee sure won't like it."

"Two of them got stood up at my place!"

Justin Boyle's voice cut over the Van Aalsts'.

"I tell you, gents, the U. P. likes it least of all. There's the three guards killed, and their money. There's the missing ten thousand in cash. And an owlhoot who maybe didn't pull the trigger, but was sure as hell there at the train the night his pards did!"

"Yeah!"

"I ask you, ain't it fitting that Whitlow's punished? What's worse than a hardcase who won't confess?"

Cain could agree with that. Since he wasn't being blamed, his mood was far from foul.

"Where's Zack Tree now?"

"Said he'd be turning in early."

"And Whitlow?"

"Safe in jail. Under watch by deputy Ike McGraw."

Justin Boyle scrubbed his chin with a forearm. "Let me see. A necktie party's out. Be morning by the time we rouse a mob." He half smiled. "Anyhow, lynching's against the law."

"What you reckon we should do, Justin?"

"Cain, you claim that our friend Zack Tree'll be ready to hang Ben Whitlow the day *after* tomorrow, but as for now, he suspicions the prisoner might be innocent. He wants to check around. But what if Thursday comes and our hangman still ain't satisfied? More delay? And here's another thing: What if Tree turns up something in Whitlow's case that'd get him released? Ben Whitlow's our man, gents; he was on the raid, I swear to it! I tracked the pretty bastard down myself! Ain't no doubt about it."

Morgan Van Aalst grunted, but it wasn't because of his too-tight vest. "It'd mean a no-account bandit getting away with murder. Freed to steal and kill again."

"Gents, here's what ought to be done," the railroad dick urged. "Bring in another hangman, maybe not with Tree's reputation, but one Red Bluff can count on to do what he's told. Getting around the country like I do, I've come to know some damned fine men like that. One, Rufus Korthaller, gets his messages relayed from Denver by telegraph. My guess is, he can start for here pronto. Let the town committee approve when his train pulls in."

Cain Van Aalst looked at Morgan Van Aalst, and the brothers solemnly nodded to one another, then to Justin Boyle. "When the dispatcher comes on duty in the morning, send a telegram. Make this Korthaller promise to rattle his hocks."

"Hell, gents," Boyle said with an authentic grin. "*I* can work the key." He strode across the depot floor. "I'll get the wire off to those who'll contact Korthaller right now."

Tree came awake in bed alert. He blinked his eyes against the streaming morning sun while he fisted the Captain Jack. With a kick and a fling, he was clear of the bedclothes, crouching low and rattlesnake deadly, the pocket pistol cocked and ready.

"Mr. Tree! Land o' Goshen!" cried Ann

Johnson, jumping two inches. The landlady nearly dropped her feather duster.

"Mrs. Johnson!"

The pair stared at each other in the middle of the room for a few seconds, the shock both parties had had thrust upon them evaporated, and they relaxed. Tree lowered the hammer of the .45, then holstered it and worked at stuffing his shirttail in his trousers. She smoothed her apron. "Good gracious, Mr. Tree, I had the notion that you'd went out. Early, you know, same as yesterday."

"Quite all right, ma'am. No harm done. You didn't surprise me undressed."

"If you choose to sleep in your daytime clothes, I'm sure it's all right with me, Mr. Tree. I can iron out wrinkles as that's needed for the sake of neatness. Just you ask, mind."

"Much obliged." If she was mystified why he slept ready for action, too bad. He wasn't about to tell her that her house had been watched by hardcases.

Mrs. Johnson took a step back and tripped hard against his traveling bag. "Oh!" The black leather case tipped over, spilling out its contents.

He expected her to act revolted—most females would be—but she surprised him. "Some spare clothes, a fresh boiled shirt— And . . . why, Mr. Tree, here's coils of rope! Hanging rope, I'll warrant!" Her eyes were round as copper pennies.

"Three-quarter-inch hemp, five-strand. All

prestretched. Inmates at a Kansas prison do it for me, special ordered. The warden's a friend; claims to admire my work"

"Ooh! What can these say?" She held up one of the square sheets, squinting from it to the hangman, smiling. "'I do hereby authorize you to hang—' And here's a blank space to be filled in by handwriting."

"I insist on an official signed instruction before stringing up a culprit."

"And this other one's a receipt form for money?"

"Coin or dust. I only take gold in payment."

"Yes, today's the hanging." The bright eyes clouded. "The one Red Bluff's been waiting for. And my husband's killer is all set to swing."

"Well, Ben Whitlow's hanging, it's been put off—"

"Indeed? Why? Why in the world— Oh!" She was staring past the hangman's shoulder. He turned and looked out the window himself.

It was the pimpled errand runner, and the kid was moving their way at a lope. He disappeared from view, and there was a clomping on the porch with a series of urgent knocks. Tree was right behind the flustered landlady when she yanked open the door.

"Is Zachariah Tree hereabouts? Oh, there you be, Mr. Hangman! The sheriff, he done sent me! You're to get down to the jailhouse, and shake a leg!"

Chapter Nine

Damned good boot-repair job, Zack Tree thought idly, picking them up and laying them down along the boardwalk toward the heart of town.

People had crowded into the main street around the cluster of important town businesses, and the way became slower going as a matter of course. There was loud grumbling, interspersed with curses, and more than one shout demanding action on the jailbreak. It was the usual reaction of frustrated citizens that Tree had heard before in communities from the Missouri to the Rio Grande. All it took to get folks' goat was an offender's slipping through the law's wide net.

Downright miscarriages of justice that punished innocent men and women just didn't seem to have the same impact.

Tree knew better than to climb on a stump and announce his doubt that Ben Whitlow had robbed a train or shot the express-car guards. The fact that the prisoner chose to escape told the whole story.

Not to Zachariah Tree, it didn't. The way he figured it, it was natural for a condemned feller to rabbit, given the chance.

In front of the Colorado Hotel, Tree was jostled by excited ribbon clerk types; in passing the noisy Silver Slipper he got in the way of rowdy cowpunchers. Between the barbershop and the livery, off-shift U. P. conductors and brakemen were spoiling for a brawl, and Roy, the stableman, had his hands full fending off would-be mount borrowers. He didn't have enough animals to go around.

"We need the broncs to hunt th' jailbreak killer!" a man shouted.

"Yeah," he was seconded. "Whitlow, th' coyote!"

"We're gonna ride the son of a bitch down and, by God, peel the hide offa his bones!"

"Fellers," Roy responded, "you pays your money, you rents your broncs. But there ain't no free rides!"

Tree rushed past with a wave to plunge into the milling, swearing throng surrounding the towering gallows. "Catch Ben Whitlow" was the general outcry now. "Kick his tail from here to glory!" "We nail him again, no waiting for no fancy-pants hangman!" "Right, boys!" "Let's go get 'im!"

Why ain't Van Aalst quieting the mob? Tree wondered. But then, rounding the last corner of the scaffold's platform, the hangman nearly ran into the lawman. "I want to talk to you, Tree," Van Aalst grunted. Then he tramped past and up the gallows steps to stand, star shining, alongside the big closed trapdoor.

"Folks! Hear me now!" Red Bluff's appointed law possessed lungs like a blacksmith's bellows.

"Th' sheriff!" "Tarnation! He's mad!" "Cain, what you want we should do?"

"Boys," Sheriff Cain Van Aalst proclaimed, "me'n the duly constituted reps of justice in this here county aim to get up a whizzer of a manhunt! The law wants Ben Whitlow to swing."

The crowd rumbled, the crowd milled. From his vantage point on the scaffold steps, Tree saw more than a few guns brought out and examined. Young bloods and old-timers alike were stirred, righteous, and outraged. The hangman didn't see a face that wasn't twisted with anger.

It was going to be one hell of a big posse.

"Where'll we meet, sheriff?" came a call.

"Here!" Van Aalst answered.

"When?"

"Fetch your horses, guns, grub! We ride in a quarter of an hour!"

With that, Sheriff Van Aalst descended the

gallows, rejoined his brother the banker, and the hangman Tree. "Inside," the law dog barked.

Tree went along because it would be quiet inside the jailhouse. And knowing the posse leaders' plans should help him play his private hand. Inside, the first object in view was the slouched deputy, Ike McGraw, behind the old oak desk. He wore a plaster on his temple like an award of honor. His expression was pained and glum.

"Tree, to fill you in on what happened," the sheriff said, "there you see the victim of that mad-dog culprit's rampage to get out. Deputy Ike took a solid hit from a clubbed six-gun."

"Who wielded the six-gun?"

"The prisoner, Benjamin Whitlow."

Tree sidled between the sheriff and the seated deputy, and back into the lockup area. No sense missing the opportunity to find out everything he could, firsthand. The door to the cell that had been occupied by the condemned man now stood wide. The small, barred window gave the same limited amount of light, but a lot more fresh air. One of the panes was broken, leaving a jagged row of sharp glass points. The floor was littered by a pile of splintered shards.

Tree walked straight in and scanned the ceiling and walls and floor. Pursing his lips he queried, "You found Ben's helper, Sheriff? It's clear as hell where the gun came from. Passed in. There tracks out back?"

"No tracks. No accomplice seen or caught. Whitlow called McGraw, showed the hogleg, and got the drop. Forced the deputy to unlock, then clubbed the poor son of a bitch." Cain Van Aalst shook his head, annoyed. "I found him when I come in this morning. Still out, lying right over there."

"In the aisle in front of the cells?"

"Tree, if you hadn't lollygagged and performed the goddamn hanging soon's you got to town . . ."

Tree was already moving back into the office area that contained the other two men. "I know what you're going to say, but it's nothing but shit. The gallows wasn't finished till late yesterday."

"Mr. Tree's right," Morgan put in.

"Uh, I did remember that."

Turning to McGraw, Tree asked the deputy, "Whitlow had the gun when you went back to the cell. What did he say?"

"That he'd shoot my balls off if I didn't turn him loose. I turned him loose, then he hit me."

"You heard nothing outside, not the glass breaking?" Tree asked.

Ike shook his head. "So Ike ain't alert like me," Cain responded. "I gave him hell for it."

By now the noise in the street had become louder. So loud that the sounds penetrated the thick jailhouse walls: shouts, horses' drumming hooves, the ringing of the firebell. The whistle and roar of a U. P. engine pulling out of the depot gave Tree a notion. "Ben's left town? He didn't catch a train?"

"No train. A puncher's bronc is missing from

the Bijou's hitch rail. We aim to follow that animal and its rider, Tree. Follow them if the trail leads to hell!"

"What if you catch Ben?"

Cain Van Aalst shrugged. "Decide when we've et that apple. Me'n Justin."

"The railroad dick's in on it?"

"Natural as ticks on hogs."

"Sheriff, I got my doubts Ben Whitlow ever killed a man or robbed a train."

"Hah!"

The door flew open with a crash. Justin Boyle made his entrance. The detective had adorned himself for posse work: brown twill trousers stuffed into mule-ear boots, a leather short jacket, and a Stetson covering the bright-gray thatch. Tree eyed him as he swaggered forward, his gaze drawn downward to his waist level. There rode a brace of what looked like brand-new pistols. A waxed, hand-tooled holster rode at each hip. U. P.'s pride hadn't worn the like at the meeting the day they'd met.

"Howdy, Cain. Morgan. Tree."

"Howdy," Morgan said.

"Glad you're here," grunted the sheriff.

"Roy'll fetch Rex out front. Then, Sheriff, we'll take the posse out. Fine horse, that Rex. He'll chase down Whitlow to the murdering bastard's death."

"You ought to bring the fugitive in alive," Zack Tree told Boyle. "I'm willing to wait around Red Bluff till you do. No extra on my fee."

The detective swiveled his head. "Didn't you tell him yet, Cain? Well, let me have the pleasure." He grinned. "Tree, you're relieved. The town has sent for Rufus Korthaller. Let a *real* hangman step in where you've done nothing but drag your feet."

And his hand flew to his holsters, dragging out the two bright, new weapons.

"What the hell—?"

"Oh, never fear, Cain," Boyle told the sheriff. "Just practicing the old draw." The dick delayed putting the guns away, however, finally doing so with some show as well as care.

If Tree's eyes served correctly, Boyle's new six-guns were the Schofield Smith and Wesson's .45. Not long on the market. The fancy butt plates carved in a steer-head design that Tree had never seen before. Custom.

So the railroad dick had two weaknesses: expensive clothes and weapons. Tree, never impressed by weaknesses, retained a poker face. "Korthaller?"

"Korthaller."

"Korthaller's a butcher."

"You're getting the idea, Tree."

A gunshot went off in the street, and then there were a few more. Rough men's voices were chanting drunkenly: "King Lynch! King Lynch!"

"Time to get the posse under way. No tracks to try and follow this time. We'll start out by combing the hills."

"Tree, I take it you ain't volunteering?" Boyle's remark was nine-tenth sneer.

"Seeing you off's likely all I can stomach."

The crowd greeted Boyle and Van Aalst by a round of cheers. Horses were brought up. The sheriff mounted, and Ike did, too. Justin Boyle found his animal a bit more trouble; the spirited stallion danced and tried to bite. Dapple gray, coal black tail and mane. Close coupled; big at over fifteen hands. Tree said to Roy, who had ambled over, "Devil horse."

"Ain't owned Rex long, has Mr. Boyle," the dark-skinned livery stableman confided. "Don't see may *paso finos* here. Mex breed. Cost a mint."

"Yo, men!" whooped the sheriff. "Let's ride!"

The posse galloped off across the railroad with more than twenty strong, shouting.

Now that the confusion in the street had calmed considerably, the rest of the crowd—women, children, and men too aged to attempt brash posse action—quickly started to melt away as well. Some merchants and tradesmen hadn't accompanied Van Aalst, Boyle, and their hard-riding crew; these kept their doors open wide and even gained the benefit of a few customers. Zachariah Tree leaned against the new gallows and let his thoughts run over the events of the last few hours.

Ben Whitlow had broken jail and lit a shuck. His accomplice disappeared. And the town had

hired Rufus Korthaller as the replacement hangman, in case Whitlow happened to survive the
manhunt. Korthaller was the most brutal paid
executioner in the West.

Tree calmly regarded Roy the liveryman, who
had walked up to him when the crowd dis-
persed.

"Hot day," Roy commented. He shot a mean-
ingful sidelong glance. "You gonna take the
black gelding out, then?"

A nod. "I reckon."

They walked over to the sprawling barn's
broad set of doors. The not-unpleasant smells of
sweet hay and fresh manure tickled the hangman's nostrils. It was a clean and well-kept
stable. "I'll go fetch your animal right on out,
then. That's your saddle over there on the stall
rail—"

"Roy, you must know the country hereabouts."

"Better'n most."

"I'm needing a different route, a back way
that can get me to the Double W."

A shark look. "That's the Whitlows' spread."

"And I don't want to run afoul of the posse.
Shit, Roy, you're their friend, I may as well tell
you. I don't figure Ben is guilty of anything but
running. Now, if his pa helped with the break
from jail, they both could be holed up close to
home. That's why—"

"You're ridin' to the ranch to find old Caleb?
You're guessing that he's the one as passed Ben
in the gun?"

"The only story that makes sense, Roy."

"The guess is plumb wrong!" The liveryman gestured with a dark-skinned hand and led the way, shuffling through the floor straw back among the stalls. Here the scents were stronger, the dimness more enveloping. Several horses snorted; one thumped a stall door with a hoof.

"Shoulda laid a bet on't, but I'm a fool," Roy grumbled. And then they came to a bale-stacked, backmost corner. "There!"

From a messed and blood-flecked bed of hay peered up a familiar face, now pouch eyed and dazed. Old Caleb Whitlow was feeling far from well. The weathered face was swollen and bore numerous scrapes and cuts.

"Caleb was walking in the street last evening," Roy explained. "His son being hanged today 'n' all, he had him a raft of gloom to carry. Then a passel of vengeance-bent railroaders jumped him and dished a beating. He barely fought clear and made it here to hide."

"Then?"

"Caleb Whitlow wasn't outta my sight after nine o'clock or so, not till morning! If somebody helped Ben bust out of jail, it sure's hell weren't this poor old man!"

Chapter Ten

Tree's stomach had the notion that his throat had been cut, and was rumbling like a canyon river rapids. The hangman strode for the cafe as a place to chew on things a spell and sit over a platter of eggs with bannock. The old man's face bore the marks of the set-to that had been described, so Roy's tale seemed brick-privy solid and honest.

The senior Whitlow had said it was true: "You b'lieve *I* busted Ben from jail? Then, Mr. Hangman, you just don't know shit!"

Tree was inclined to agree that he'd guessed dead wrong about young Ben's accomplice in escape. But then, damn it, who *had* smashed the window and passed the six-gun through into the condemned man's cell?

But he understood one thing, and it was the

degree to which Ben Whitlow was generally hated. The U. P. robbery had cut Red Bluff deep. Those slain guards had been popular men.

On the cafe threshold, Tree was bumped by a jasper hurrying out. Girlish of build, although wearing a suit and a perky waxed mustache, he let his face flow swiftly from blank to very bright indeed.

"Begging your pardon, I'm in a rush," Tree muttered.

"Say! Ain't you the famous 'Hanging' Tree?" The sissified fellow's arms came up. He hurled away a birchwood toothpick.

"Name's Zachariah Tree, if it matters."

"Oh, it matters, Mr. Tree! To Jethro Randolph of the Chronicle! To the world!"

"Like I said, I got me a busy day. Now—"

A pad came from Randolph's inside pocket. "Since I run into you this way, Zack, perhaps a quick interview? The week's edition goes to press soon's I sashay back to the office. Big story, this, the jailbreak. What now, since your victim has skedaddled? Gone scat!"

"Now see here, Randolph. I reckon you was down by the gallows this morning, listened yourself to the sheriff's words, watched the posse ride out. To me, that's at least a couple of stories to put in print."

"But, Tree! Bundles of papers will go out on the afternoon train! You owe it to your wide public—"

"No statement! No, thanks!"

If the reporter was roughly brushed aside, it was because he was in the way.

Two minutes later Zachariah Tree was wolfing down hot coffee laced with potent chicory. The cafe lady with the grease-splashed apron was saying, "Don't pay mind to Jethro Randolph. He's like a donkey; don't bray, but Lordy, do he like to talk. . . ."

The bright, large kitchen was filled with heat and the aroma of baking bread when Morgan Van Aalst stormed in. The banker's tiny porcine eyes shone dangerously. "Damn it, where's my desk-drawer six-gun? You know the one I mean, Josie! The Walker forty-four!"

The wife turned from the cookstove and pushed back a golden tendril. Above the gingham housedress, her face flushed pink. She didn't speak.

"Woman, are you deaf? I said—" He broke off his words, suddenly suspicious. "I wanted to check the loads today. I didn't ride with the posse—got business here in town—but that killer Whitlow's escaping makes a man like to be prepared for anything."

The woman's response was a rigid jaw set, nothing more.

"What's got into you, woman?"

Silence.

The big man's hammy paw shot out and grabbed her by the shoulder. A few violent jerks, and the woman was being shaken the way a terrier shakes a rat. She was biting her lip, and a crimson bead of blood popped in a corner of her mouth.

Morg Van aalst was a big man, and he possessed a good deal of strength. Now his massive head jutted forward on his bullneck as his words hissed out. "We got to go over old ground again, gal? What I promised the very hour after we stood in front of the preacher? I said I'd be the boss in my own house!" As he gripped her, he slapped her face hard with his free hand. She gasped. He struck her again.

"No, Morg! No!"

This time he clutched a breast through the cloth and gave it a sharp twist. Then he pushed her away, and she fetched up hard against the canary yellow wall. "I come in to talk to you, and you wear that goddamn smirk! Well, I'll wipe it off your face, like I done before!" He jerked her arm, digging with spatula-like fingers. The woman yelped and fell beside the kindling box. The husband towered over her, glowering.

"P-please, Morg? I've done nothing!"

"A woman must be shown her place! And remember my other wedding-day vow! I find you've lain with another man, that's the very hour I'll wring your pretty neck! Believe that!"

There was the sound of low sobs. Morg Van Aalst turned on his booted heel. "I'll be upstairs with the ledgers I brought home. I aim to work on them till evening. Get yourself together, woman. This house is a pigpen. Clean it!"

After her husband had stomped out, Josie huddled for a long while, unable to stir. Then the hurt from her bruises subsided some, but she couldn't stop crying. Morg was good at keeping promises. Too good. She had lived with his threats, knowing his vengeful nature, sure that he'd find her if she fled.

Lord, but she was scared to die!

Ben Whitlow urged the leggy roan that he straddled up yet another long, steep incline deep in mountain fastness. Since riding out of Red Bluff twelve hours earlier he'd pressed the stolen mount pretty hard. He'd still been in the low foothills, though, when dawn's pink flush began to color the eastern sky. He'd kept due north as the murky web of darkness faded and gave way to brightness, then he turned the animal's nose west on a heading for the heart of the tall Wind River saw-tooths.

By now the going could be called badlands travel. The land was crisscrossed with gullies and tortuous canyons. So soon in the year there was still enough snow runoff to swell the watercourses, making wide detours from any straight-way planned route necessary.

Maybe he'd never make Idaho, the way he planned, the fugitive thought grimly.

The roan topped the notch, and Whitlow reined to permit it to blow. Ahead the magnificent peaks loomed, and Whitlow scanned the timber-locked slopes. The going would become still rougher in the hours and days to come, and not the least of his problems was bound to be food. Oh, there'd be forage aplenty for the galled and worn-out plug that wore the Circle Bar brand—the only one he'd found saddled at the saloon hitch rail. But it was his own stomach that was already giving him the hunger growls.

He couldn't stop to try and shoot a rabbit or bird. The six-gun he'd been passed, he'd found out, was empty of cartridges.

Nor was there any grub—not even jerked beef—in the saddlebags. Or even a scrap of fishline, much less hooks.

He let the horse crop trail-side grass for another minute, then lifted his eyes to scan the sky. Mare's-tail clouds wisped the vast blue dome, and a high speck of a buzzard coasted.

"All right, bronc, giddap." He toed the mount's sides stocking footed, and it moved out trotting, still well fed, not tired.

Not usable firearm, no grub but wild berries he might spot, no boots. One hell of a well pulled-off run for freedom. He had no doubt there was a posse in pursuit, riled to nail his hide up. His only advantage was that they wouldn't know which way he'd come.

Unless in combing, they cut his trail, and the shoes of the Circle Bar bronc were recognized.

Unless Josie was found out and forced to talk. He'd told her his intent to make for Boise.

Ben guided the gelding down a boulder-strewn stretch that ended in a piñon grove. He was getting too weary to keep up the pace. He was going to need rest. He stepped from leather and flopped on some shady mountain-meadow grama. He fell asleep quickly.

As he dozed, the sun had westerned considerably, drawing the blessed pine shade from him, and dazzling his eyes. Ben Whitlow rolled over and spotted the ground-hitched roan not far off. In the bout of fitful slumber he'd somehow dreamed, and now, dry mouthed, he sat up to ponder. Josie Van Aalst took a big risk on his behalf, snatching Morgan's gun and sneaking through the dark to the jail. Maybe she was in danger now because of it.

But then, hadn't he been the one in danger, facing hanging all those many past days—and on her account? Saying nothing of the fact that he'd spent the twenty-eighth with her in her husband's absence. Letting the trail drag through, letting him self be convicted of train robbing, murder.

Morgan Van Aalst could have killed his Josephine, and would have been permitted to get away scot-free. Morgan Van Aalst's brother was the sheriff for hundreds of square miles around Red Bluff.

His muscles aching from hours spent in the saddle, Ben Whitlow labored to his feet and limped down to the stream. He splashed chilly water on his stubble-shaddowed face, drank, and felt better. Swinging aboard, he kicked up the roan and put it to a trot . . . then reined to a halt again. Every hour was four or so more miles put between him and Josie.

Perhaps Josie would never be able to meet him in the Idaho gold camps as they'd planned.

A breastwork of thunderclouds had mounted above the peaks, alive with forked lightning; arrowing, ominous. Like his chances. He wheeled the horse around and set it back the way they'd come. All he'd need to do was avoid the posse, play his cards right, and he'd be in his Josie's arms real soon.

The devil take the posse and that bastard Justin Boyle.

The fierce, hazy white Nevada sky flung down heat with the force of a giant fist. Arroyo City and its inhabitants simmered on an immense griddle under the onslaught of the wind. In a crowd, it was worst of all, and the broad single street of the town was filled with men and women. In the absence of shade trees, people hugged the few adobe building walls to escape the hot sun.

At the west end of the business district soared a new raw-lumber gallows. On the crossbeam, two stiff nooses were strung. As of yet, the nooses remained empty.

The crowd had been waiting for hours, since the appointed death time of the Barton cousins was by now well past.

Still, the spectators declined to leave, or even temporarily abandon vantage points, positions scuffled over and hard won. Reve and Lyle Barton's capture and conviction for manslaughter had taken the lives of some good men. The outlaws were sly, cunning, and familiar with the desert. That pair had robbed a silver claim, taken a miner's mule to pack the loot, and killed the old miner.

But where the hell was the bald, ugly, hog-fat-and-buffalo-stinking noose man, Rufus Korthaller? the mob in the street began muttering. "Was from saloon to saloon all mornin'," said one old-timer.

His grizzled *compadre* snapped, "Shore. 'Twas."

"Last evenin's banquet at the mayor's, up past midnight, buckin' tiger at th' Gamblers' Strike." "Seen him m'self, by jingo!" "In Mrs. Lulu's hat shop, where the whores go." "Bought hisself a paper rose for his damned lapel."

The grumbling reached a shouting level. "Where's Rufus Korthaller? Where's the hangman what Arroyo City hired?"

"Don't want no more printed cards of th' culprits' wrote-out history, at a nickel apiece!"

"Poor printin' job, anyways!" "Don't want no more peddlers hawkin' rope bits from Korthaller's last job!"

A kid with a souvenir-laden neck tray veered aside and into an alley.

"We want Korthaller!" "Hell, we want Reve and Lyle Barton! Fetch out the cousins!"

A reporter scribbled with a pencil stub.

"Soiled Dove" Sal swigged deeply from a flask brought out of her skirts.

"Hangman! Hangman!"

At the end of the street, a rising murmur could be heard: the east end opposite the stout, tall gallows. The sound multiplied in the stifling air. There was a steady *clop-clop* of four slow-moving hooves. "Hey, there!" There was a buckboard under way coming from the jail, carrying the prisoners.

On the sprung seat ahead of the caged, bound Barton cousins, sat two men, the driver and another. The man not fisting the reins wore a loud checked suit, a derby hat, and split shoes of lizard. The paper rose pinned over his heart was dyed a bright calf's-tongue pink.

The hangman lifted his heavy jowls in a grin, and waved with fingers the shape of sausages.

"Hurrah! Hurrah!" surged the crowd, making way, then closing behind the short, macabre cavalcade. "Rufus Korthaller!" "The Uplift Society's finest!"

"Hoist 'em high, Rufus!" a trio of placer miners whooped in unison. "Don't be nobody deserves th' big swing more'n them no-count Bartons!"

Five minutes later the hard-luck kinsmen stood together on the scaffold's low, flat platform. Under each pair of feet was a heavy trap ready to be sprung. The men, one young and hairy, the other middle-aged, were collared with thick rope, both slip knots drawn, angling behind an ear. The Barton's hands were tied in front and both pairs of thighs were trussed tight above trembling knees.

"Will she go fast, Lyle?" the younger whispered.

"Just dunno, boy. Th' goddamn drop don't look very long to this child's eyes."

Rufus Korthaller was a short man, and obscenely fat. His chins overflowed the collar of his tent-sized shirt. When he swabbed sweat from his hairless crown, it gleamed cue-ball round, cue-ball shining. Now he smiled with dingy, crooked teeth and gusted a foul-breathed snort. "Any last words, culprits? No? Then hell's bells, let 'er rip!"

Korthaller's vicious yank on a lever activated the trap mechanism, and the weighted doors boomed like miniature cannon. But absent were the pistol-loud pops that would have signaled cleanly breaking necks. In the great hush that had come over the crowd, were heard hideous gurglings and the gagging of strangulation instead. The writhing, kicking, twisting forms of both victims were clearly seen, partly above the floor, partly below, through the open platform front. Blood covered both men's shirts, and spouted from their noses, mouths, and ears. Eyeballs bulged. Voiding bladders and bowels filled the air with an acrid stench.

The Barton boys' necks both stretched three inches. Convulsions seized the men, agonizing, severe.

The minutes dragged on. The men went on twitching at the ropes' ends. The gurglings

110

turned more faint. A few cheers broke from the spectators and grew in frenzy and volume to encompass the seething square. Overhead, the sky blazed. On the scaffold Rufus Korthaller slurped whiskey passed to him in a jug. And then a youth leaped up the steps and thrust a flimsy telegraph into the fat hangman's hand. "A wire, Mr. Korthaller! Just come over the company's key!"

"Well, well, well . . ." The greasy lips pursed. Scanning the telegram, Korthaller smiled wider while the Bartons continued to labor and writhe.

A lawman at his elbow asked, "Bad news?"

"Goddamn! No! Quite the opposite! Another job's waiting, is all this here message tells Rufus."

And then, in a lower-pitched voice he asked, "When's the next stage leave for Red Bluff, Wyoming Territory?"

Chapter Eleven

Zachariah Tree hurled aside a copy of the *Chronicle*, got up from the cafe table and the remains of his breakfast, and strode to the door. Stepping out into the chilly morning drizzle, he surveyed the low, leaden sky. Likely to keep up a few hours, he decided, even though the brunt of the cloudburst had blown through Red Bluffs after midnight.

Almost twenty-four hours from the time that Ben Whitlow was being handed a six-gun through a window cell window and breaking jail.

The local newspaper's account of the "daring escapade" had filled most of the front page, and as a bonus also retold the story of the cold-blooded U. P. holdup murders. Young Whitlow was called the "Fiery-haired devil"; such a hardened criminal that he'd refused to tell identities of his gang, where they'd gone, or what had happened to the missing ten thousand in gold.

Old stuff, but there was something new, too—a tidbit had gone unmentioned to Tree by Van Aalst and Justin Boyle.

A reward was being offered for the killer: $1500 for the man who brought Ben Whitlow in—dead or alive.

Tree headed for the livery stable, but behind his stern poker face, his brain raced locomotive fast and furiously. If Tree could find Ben first, he might convince the fool to reveal his alibi and his accomplice, and no longer take the blame for the long-gone unknown owlhoots who'd really robbed the train.

Now the rain was coming down harder, dancing in the puddles of the muddy, deserted street. In a minute he'd be at the livery, where Roy would have lit the monkey stove. After partial drying-out for a while, Tree would saddle the black and don the heavy oilcloth slicker for the ride on up into the hills. If it turned out that Ben was holed up on Double W land, he might find him before the posse did.

Then the notion hit Tree. He stopped stock-still in the rain and wondered, Who had put up the reward? The sum was more than most men earned in a whole four years. Would the railroad be so free to buy revenge? Recovering the loot seemed a lost cause. Most companies didn't throw good money after bad.

Tree turned on his heel and splashed back the way he'd come. In that direction lay the bank run by one Morgan Van Aalst.

The knock at the front door brought Josie Van Aalst off the parlor divan and onto trim feet in front of the mantel pier glass to size her reflection. Her hair was a rich wine yellow in the glow of a lamp on this rainy spring day; her gaunt cheeks were somewhat flushed from sitting close to the fire.

She smoothed her dress with hands that trembled slightly, then moved to the front entryway, with it's large brass cupid, and drew open the door. "Yes?" Distaste soured her features further. As if she hadn't enough to put up with!

"Howdy," Zachariah Tree said blandly. "Mrs. Van Aalst, I take it? My name's Tree. Be obliged to talk to your husband, ma'am."

She peered past him at the downpour, then her gaze fixed his streaming face. "Morgan is—"

"Here. They told me at the bank that he was."

"Is that so?"

"Yep. Uh . . . begging your pardon, ma'am, it's powerful wet out in this rain."

"All right, come in. Wipe your boots"—he was doing so—"and I'll go call Morgan." She stepped through an archway and out of sight.

She returned within a minute. "My husband says, through the speaking tube in his study, that I'm to show you into the parlor. Will you come this way?"

The parlor was a big fancy room with a rug underfoot, thick enough to sprain your ankle, and crimson drapes. The blazing hearth log did help to dry a body, though, Tree thought.

"You may take a seat," Josie Van Aalst said crisply.

"I'd as soon stand, ma'am."

"Suit yourself."

She glided to a corner, her skirt rustling to her dainty step. There she stood, heavy lidded, still pouting, her red, bee-stung lips turned down in disapproval.

"Begging your pardon for missing last night's shindig, ma'am. Got your invite late. I ain't the sociable kind, I fear."

"Oh, Mr. Tree, the gathering was my husband's idea. I confess I wasn't disappointed much. You'll excuse my coolness toward your profession."

"Needs doing in these times. Your husband's town committee was the ones as brought me here."

"To put a man to death. I know."

"Folks die—plenty of them—every single day."

"Not choked before their natural time with a rope."

He was about to tell her that the culprits *he* dealt with didn't choke, that the long drop snapped the vertebrae, and that death was accomplished in an instant. But then the lady's husband was in the room. Advancing grim faced, he glared at Tree.

"So, you see fit to come under my roof, after all. A change from yesterday, Tree?"

"I already excused myself to the lady. This here's another matter, Van Aalst, and I'd be beholden for your cooperation. Nobody else I know of is in town to ask, your brother and Justin Boyle off to do their duty."

"On the posse. Yes, of course. I couldn't go myself because—"

"No excuse required." Tree came straight to the point. "Van Aalst, I read in the town paper that there's a reward offered for Ben Whitlow—dead or alive." Behind him he heard the woman's faint gasp, but he rushed on. "I'm curious to know where the fifteen hundred's going to come from."

The heavier, stouter man thrust blunt thumbs into the armholes of his waistcoat and rocked back and forth. The slab face looked even more hostile than it had a minute ago, as the banker seemed to firm up a resolve. "I don't see as the reward's any of your concern, Tree," he snapped. "You dragged your feet on hanging Whitlow and got fired off the job. But if you must know, the Union Pacific offered the reward. Mr. Boyle will distribute it when the man is brought in. Now, I'm a busy man, with no more time to waste. My wife will show you out."

With that, Morg Van Aalst tramped from the

room. Soon his heavy tread could be heard on the hall stairs.

Tree let the lady of the house escort him to the entryway. There she stopped abruptly and hissed out in a whisper, "Is it true you delayed the execution? Then you aren't the brutal beast I thought!" All at once she was half smiling, but then her arm brushed the cupid statue and she winced.

"Ma'am, you're injured?"

"I-it's nothing." But the shawl she had draped herself with had slipped, exposing her forearm. A purple bruise ran from wrist to elbow. Then her hand fled to the bruise on her cheek.

The hangman nodded and slammed on his hat. He felt her eyes on his back all the way down the path. Well, he'd gained two pieces of information: about the U. P., and about Morgan Van Aalst, as well.

He might have suspected that, besides the rest, the bastard was a wife beater.

The sky was still a dripping, lead gray blanket as Tree slogged toward town through deepening mud and puddles. Fewer people than even an hour earlier now moved about in Red Bluff; an occasional pedestrian, an occasional hunched-over horseman, no wagons or carriages at all. Only the railroad seemed to have traffic as usual; down on the tracks stood a train, and off the train straggled passenger arrivals. Their distance- and rain-blurred small forms scuttled and scattered, some for refuge in the depot, some, the stauncher, bound for businesses or homes. A few indistinct shapes disappeared into the Bijou, and the hangman judged them the wisest of the lot.

Being closer to the larger, more conspicuously false-fronted Silver Slipper, he headed that way. Shoving through the bat-wings, he found himself surprised and in a crowd.

Townsmen, ranchers, and railroaders thronged the bar three deep. Gamblers filled rear tables. A piano thumped out "Buffalo Gals," never one of Zack Tree's favorites.

The hangman elbowed his way close to a sweating, aproned bar dog. The fellow cocked an eye toward the newcomer clothed in black.

"Beer."

"Right." The man produced from under the heavily waxed mahogany counter an uncorked bottle. Zang's, the label read, all the way from La Junta, Colorado. "That'll be one nickel, mister."

As he swigged and thought about the U. P.'s reward, it did make sense somehow that the U. P. would post money for a culprit their own already caught. Seemed like good money after bad to him.

Just then he noticed a familiar bespectacled face in the polished back-bar mirror. It belonged to the night dispatcher from the depot. The man he'd seen in the dazzling acetylene glare the evening of the first powwow he'd had with Boyle.

118

Shoving his way down along the bar, Tree shouldered through a clutch of U. P. gandy dancers. Heavy whiskey drinkers all, they scarcely looked up from their glasses and half-drunk bottle. "Pardon me, gents. Pardon me." The next obstacle was a trifle harder, in the person of a flirting glitter gal. "Buy me a drink, big boy?"

"Feller over there's bigger still. Best ask him." At last the hangman stood beside the depot man, who, it happened, appeared cold sober and grouchy to boot.

"Howdy."

"Howdy."

"Terrible thing, Ben Whitlow's escape," Tree observed. "As a railroad man, you got to be damned riled. I know I am."

"Damn right!" the man squinted into Tree's face. "Hey, ain't you the hangman?"

"True. But that don't change the deaths of three fine men."

"Rusty Baylock, a stone loafer. Hank Jones, a violator of old Rule G, pertainin' to drinkin' on the job." The dispatcher used the spittoon, smacked his lips, and continued. "Onliest jasper in that express-car bunch worth the knowin'—randy Hubert Johnson. Hell of a guy, but lock up your missus and daughters. Catch my drift?" An elbow to Tree's rib cage.

"That kind, hey? Well, decent of the railroad, though, putting up the reward for the man as done them in."

The wiry man turned full face to Zack Tree,

screwed his eyes up, and the slack mouth, too. "Where'n tarnation you hear that one? The U. P.'s cheap, Mr. Hangman. The shebang's run for the profits of them on top. Mogul Durant kitty up for a reward? Hangman, you've ate loco weed!"

"But—"

An outburst in the rear of the saloon was kicking up a flurry of curses and loud yells. A table went over with a crash, and the slick-haired barkeep nervously clutched a bung starter. Tree's and the dispatcher's eyes were drawn like magnets to the fracas, now spreading like wildfire. A tall man in a trail-stained buck-skin shirt was at the center of it, trading blows with six or eight others.

"Goddamnit," someone roared. "Rita-Sue, she's my gal! Don't truck with saddle-tramp scum!"

"And all us Slocums back our brother Homer!"

"Club the bucksin shirt! Kick his woman-stealin' ass!"

The tall man took a gut punch and staggered back against the bar. Tree peered into the lean, black-mustached face with the sinister scarred eyebrow. His eyebrow twitched. "Milt? Milt Henley?"

"Tree?"

Tree glimpsed the flash of a derringer's blunt barrel in the hand of Homer. He kicked high, and the weapon spun away.

"Hell, I can't believe it," Milt Henley blurted.

"In a tight, and here you be, Zack! Old *amigo*—"

"Look out!"

The massed bunch of Slocum brothers charged.

Chapter Twelve

The man with the scarred left eyebrow had ridden into Red Bluff from the west, his short-coupled steel-dust mare splashing the muddy street. His Dakota-creased tall hat was sodden, and so was the buckskin shirt under the yellow oilcloth slicker. He'd deposited his horse, saddle, and Winchester at the Negro stableman's barn, pausing only to remove a folded sheet of newspaper from his saddlebag to stuff into his pocket. Told of the sheriff's absence at the jailhouse office by a pimply kid, the lean man had cursed vilely and asked if the reward still stood.

"For Ben Whitlow? Stranger, I ain't sure, but if I was you, I'd go ask in the saloons. Folks in there, there are, knows most things. You a bounty hunter?"

"Ee-yeah."

"Go and try the Silver Slipper."

So he'd wiped his mustache with his sleeve, loosened his matched Remington six-guns in their holsters, and ducked back out into the rain.

The Slipper's side entrance was the closest, and near the door he'd taken a vacant table.

He hadn't stayed alone long.

The misunderstanding over the big-busted glitter gal resulted from almost nothing. She'd brought his whiskey order and lingered to flirt. He'd responded. Hell, who wouldn't?

The explosion of the hardcase crew of Slocums had come with tornado speed: first they weren't there, then they were. He'd refrained from shooting, since a man couldn't hunt wanted fellers, locked in a cell himself.

So, he'd been punched and hurled into the bar. And when he looked up, he saw Zack Tree.

After he kicked aside the derringer, it seemed to be raining Slocum brothers. There was a thrown chair, and the back-bar mirror dissolved in shards. At his side, Zachariah Tree punched a Slocum, flinging him into the other Slocums, howling with rage and pain.

The bounty hunter vented his own rebel yell, and waded back into the fray. The Slocums were joined by friends, but to no avail. Henley flailed with a fist. A man fell away with a ruined nose.

The stirred-up townsmen lost no time in closing in, cutting off retreat. Tree was occupied battling two mean, grizzly giants who wanted to kick and gouge. Henley absorbed a swipe to the side of his head, shook it off, and retaliated with a gut punch.

Then, out of the blue, he called out, "Tree! Behind you!"

The hangman, turning, raised his fierce gray gaze. "Milt? . . ."

Tree turned, saw the looming lummox, and drove bunched knuckles to his breastbone, hurling him back. The man wielding a faro layout slammed into the wall. "When'd you get in?" the hangman called over to Henley.

"Hour ago's all." Henley pumped a kick, sending a boot toe square to a charging track layer's groin. Above the painted howl he yelled: "Been long in town yourself?"

"No." A duck, a feint, a thrown lip-splitting swipe, and the enemy collapsed. "A couple days."

Henley staggered an opponent with an uppercut. "The Whitlow hanging?"

"C'rect!"

"Haw! Zack, but your pigeon has flown, by God!"

The hangman and the bounty hunter stood spraddle-legged and waded into the confused swirl of ganged-up attackers, tooth and claw. "Break their faces!" whooped one ornery Slocum. "Play with Rita-Sue, would they?" "Break their bones!" So saying, this one, a gorilla-armed, lank-haired brute, launched a roundhouse swing and connected with the jaw

124

of Milt Henley. The mustached man's eyes glazed.

But only for an instant. Powering back savagely, the bounty hunter lowered a shoulder and right-crossed the jasper with a fist to the throat. There was a brittle rattle of a crushing Adam's apple, and the man hurtled backward into a pard. "Hurt, Lafe? Take this, you bastard!" The loudmouth snatched up, and flung the keno goose. The gambling device caught Busted Voice Box in the forehead. All went down in an explosion of littered betting chips.

Meanwhile, his muscles pile-driving, Zach Tree forged toward the bar. There lay the heart of the opposition, he perceived, in a clot of swearing, swinging gandies. All were big men, sunbrowned, stubble chinned, who earned their livings by wielding pickaxes from dawn to dusk.

The rampagers were crazy-drunk. Bull-thick shoulder to bull-thick shoulder, now they ran at Tree. "And, you, hangman, helpin' the polecat what pissed-off Homer!" Tree was grabbed by a huge, hammy hand, drawn in a vicious hug.

"Attaway, Boxcar! Smash th' damned hangman's ribs!" And it was happening! Sheer agony lanced through the pressured torso. Tree's lung strained for air, and his vision blurred. The hangman's head was full of clanging church bells—and he hadn't a religious bone. As if from beyond an ocean, he heard the chorus of threatening shouts. He tried some punches. They were awkward, deflected.

And the man called Boxcar only squeezed harder.

"Hold on, Zack, I'm a-coming!" Henley, pinned in a corner, combatted odds. The town's blacksmith and its wrestling champ teamed, flailed, and kept him at bay. A sledging backhand blow from a hog-haunch forearm buckled his knees. A clublike heel rammed his groin. Hellish agony washed outward in waves from the struck spot.

Lashing out powerfully now, despite his pain, Henley gut-punched, face-smashed, and butted his way through the gang-up toward Zach. Tree, for his part, heaved mightily, threw both legs out to settle his weight, and upset the big bear hugger. As he was overbalanced, the lopsided, ugly puss was pulled down.

Tree's knuckles plowed into the man's mouth, launching a spray of spit and blood down the jasper's chin and shirt. Boxcar's arms loosed, and he reeled away, colliding with the saloon's great wheel of fortune. The colorful wheel split across the middle, and the whole rig came in pieces around the flung man. Boxcar hit the floor like a felled ponderosa. Tree leaped over the twitching form to reach Henley, and as he did so, Boxcar jumped up and fled.

Suddenly the brawl seemed over; all seven of the hulking Slocum brothers, having seen the error of their ways, had run or limped off, clutching various injured body parts. In the several doorways of the saloon, bat-wings flopped back and forth on loud hinges, signaling hurried exits. The bounty hunter and the dark-clothed hangman faced each other across the open floor.

Open, but not quite empty. Huddled into a squirming, whining ball lay the very reason for the fight, the faded drink hustler and sometime dancing girl, Rita-Sue. The rice-powdered face was caked by tears, and a skinny arm dangled at grotesque angle. Tree was sure *he* hadn't done it to her. She must have stopped a blow of one of her own defenders.

A few saloon patrons and, of course, the bar dogs stood idly about, doing nothing. Tree looked at Henley. "Busted arm. Feel sorry for her?"

"Yeah."

"Me, too." Tree crouched and lifted the light, shuddering form in the flame orange dress. "There a sawbones in this Godforsaken town?" he shouted.

A coot in green galluses answered, "Not far. Office back o' th' apothecary's. Next to the jail."

"Carrying her easy?" Henley said. Tree nodded.

"I don't see how we get into these messes," the bounty man added.

"You been in Red Bluff, what? A whole hour? It just ain't the nicest place in the world."

Ben Whitlow rode like a man beaten by exhaustion—which he was. Milky rain pounded his hatless crown in sheets, the red hair plastered to his scalp like a cap of crushed brick dust. Water soaked his shirt; the pants needed wringing. Under his swaying form the horse slogged the trail, often stumbling itself from the steady, fatiguing pace.

Well, nobody said being a fugitive from a hanging was an easy life.

And, Christ, could you get hungry as hell, living it!

The surrounding peaks he'd come through in the overnight had lowered to become round hills, and now it was day, so he didn't have to go by lightning flash. But although the going was nowhere near as taxing, the damage had been done. His eyelids were heavy as anvils, and his arms and legs burned for rest. The ache in his head was a steady, knelling throb, and if there was anything he wanted to do, it was climb down and curl up to sleep. Trouble was, however, he'd been traveling for some time on quite dangerous ground. He was again crossing Double W range, too near Red Bluff to relax, too near Van Aalst country to think of shut-eye.

Unless he made it to the precise place he had in mind: a hole-up almost nobody knew of up a tiny, blind rock cut. It had dependable seep, shelter, and trappable small game. He should be safe there for a spell. Safe till word could be gotten to his Josie. And once reunited with the woman, he could reengineer escape for both of them. Escape for him from the murder charge. Escape for her from that damnable marriage.

Riding into a gully flanked with reddish,

towering boulders, Ben knew it wouldn't be long. There was less than five miles, as the crow flew, to his pa's ranch's headquarters barns. And up the yonder rock-patched slope, his hidey-hole spot.

Too bad, Sheriff, he said silently. Too bad, Justin Boyle, you sneaky, lying son of a bitch. I got your posse fooled, and I'll be sitting pretty.

And all it would take was a mite more good luck.

Chapter Thirteen

"So then, Doctor. How do you reckon it?"

In the not large but comfortably accommodated office, Zachariah Tree stood beside the leather, padded examining table. Against the wall behind him leaned the bounty hunter Henley, clothes still not quite dry from the rain, and looking poker faced behind his mustache. Under a framed diploma from an Eastern medical college, the woman Rita-Sue sat, her broken forearm neatly splinted and supported in a neck-suspended sling. Her expression registered pain as he, too, eyed the bushy-haired man with the rolled-up sleeves and skewed string tie.

Dr. Gabriel Everly had been long on the frontier. He had mended a good many broken limbs, and gained plenty in the course of bar-room fights. That could have been the reason why he looked bored. "Oh, she'll heal, and likely fast," he said gruffly. "Young and strong, the way she is. The ravages of her profession haven't yet caught up with her. You do feel better now in that splint, don't you, Rita-Sue?"

The glitter gal nodded. "Can I leave yet?"

Henley's naturally sinister look turned to surprise. "You're all that well already?"

"A gal's got to work. You figure Stacy the saloon owner pays the help if they happen to be laid up? Wrong as hell!"

Zachariah Tree shrugged and half smiled. Everly said, "You can go. Just be careful you don't knock that arm around more than you have to."

She gave a saucy toss of her henna curls. "Right, doc. I'll tell my customers." As she left, ether smells wafted stronger than lilac toilet water.

Milt Henley pushed away from the wall where he'd been leaning. "Seems a good-hearted enough gal, which is why we fetched her over after her accident. Tree, there, judged she had just a simple break."

The doctor glanced up from filling his briar pipe. "Tree. You're the hangman, then. I'll bet, your profession being what it is, you'd be a good judge of muscle tone, bone condition, and so forth. Especially regarding neck muscles and neck bones."

"It's my living doing hangings, I admit."

"Ironic. Ironic in the extreme." Dr. Everly

scratched a match and lit his pipe, his hands working steadily as if at surgery. "The idea of a living earned by killing."

Henley put in, "'Tain't so odd. My kind of trade, too."

"And you, sir, are a—?"

"Bring culprints in to collect rewards. Often as not, tied across a saddle."

"Bounty hunter?"

"Ee-yeah."

He took in a puff and blew out a cloud. "Well, can't claim that I approve. I'm a healer, I don't hold much with killing."

"Always?" Tree was by the office window now, frowning as he peered through cloudy glass. "Maybe you never cottoned to the Whitlow execution?"

"Well . . ."

"This here alley," Tree pursued. "Runs along the jailhouse. Window gives a view. Doc, it ever happen that you spend the night in this office?"

He stroked his chin. "Most nights, matter of fact. I do rent lodgings, but they're far across town."

"About the jailbreak night. When Ben Whitlow got away. Did you see who helped him?"

The doc stared and looked into Tree's eyes. "You expect an answer?"

Tree stepped close. "That tears it. You saw something, right enough."

"You came to Red Bluff to hang young Ben Whitlow! *I* oppose executions! Favor prisons to cure criminal woes!"

"Doc, I mean for you to—"

Henley's first came down on the table. "Gents! Gents!"

Two heads swiveled; the hangman's and the healer's. Both faces were screwed, determination written there. Eyes sparked. "Henley! What the hell?"

"Listen, Doc." The bounty hunter spoke fast, urgently. "Sure, Zack's a hangman. Me—well, that ain't to the point. The point is, Zack's the only hangman I know who cares a damn about justice. Won't hang the wrong man. If the condemned is guilty as sin, they swing clean, painless. But if guilt's doubtful, Tree'll move heaven and earth, work to clear good names!"

"I-I didn't realize—"

Everly joined Tree and the others at the window. "Well, I did see something, as the moon that night was full. There was a woman. Blond, I think, wearing a fancy dress. She brought a big pistol out of her skirts, smashed the jail glass, and tossed the weapon through. A few minutes later, right out there, she was joined by Whitlow. The couple kissed, then fled in different directions."

"You raised no uproar on account of the prisoner faced hanging."

The medical man made no answer.

There was a bit of triumph in Zack Tree's smile. Satisfaction in Henley's, too. "Now," Tree insisted, "so's to clear Ben, I got to have the lady's name."

"I told you all I know. I didn't recognize her."

"I'll accept your word on that point, Doc, 'cause I got to. Come on, Henley, let's get us a breath of fresh air."

"A goddamn toast!" growled the slurred voice of Justin Boyle. The campfire under the rock shelf played on his features: thin lips, nose, and long slack jaw. He glanced around at the huddled possemen, raised his tin cup, and spoke with mock solemnity. "To the early and ugly death of the murderer, Ben Whitlow—of lead poisoning!"

"Hear, hear!"

"I'll drink to that 'un, by gum!" The dough-ball greengrocer who said it slapped his rusty dragoon pistol and laughed.

The sodden day had driven the crew to the shelter, such as it was under the mountain face. Out of the wind, out of the worst downpour, the pocked overhang was a refuge, little more. Beyond the stick blaze, across a swale, lay a motte of canopying pine, elders, and oaks, where the horses were tied. At least the men were off the horses, sipping boiled Arbuckle's laced with Old Overholt from the railroad dick's flask.

The sheriff, too, nodded agreeably, and drank off his warming cupful. But the Red Bluff dry-goods store owner, a banty rooster of a man, jumped from his tailor-fashion crouch. "The son of a bitch is set to hang! The town sent for Korthaller!"

"That was before the prisoner broke jail!"

Abraham Strom's objection wilted. "Say, that's right. Plumb glad I thunk of that."

"Clouds breakin' up out west," Deputy Mc-Graw observed. "Be fit to ride afore much longer, though the rain'll have washed out any tracks we might've cut otherwise."

"Then we'll just go on looking as before," Strom declared. "I'm anxious as any man-jack to corner that mad dog! And it ain't only 'cause I served on the jury as convicted him. Any jail-breaking galoot goes against the law. We take vengeance, else we're no better than red injuns ourselves!"

After his little speech, the merchant joined other townsmen, kicking sand over the fires, tightening cinches, and tying the big cow-camp coffeepots to saddles. The first clear rays of sunlight were beaming through the clouds, and the world looked scrubbed clean, including the nearby timber-locked slopes.

"Got me a hunch, Cain," Boyle said, taking the sheriff aside. "You inclined to listen?"

"Yeah. What?"

Boyle moved close, hiking to the horses. "Looks like two ways to go from here: combing toward the north trying to overtake the bastard, or drift on back, keeping our eyes peeled all the while. But we ain't far now from the Whitlow spread. What if Ben's gone to ground there? Seems to me there's a powerful chance."

"Then, if he did head north, we'd lose him, certain."

"Appears to me we've lost him, anyways. But

the storm could've made him turn back. The storm or something else."

Cain spat. "*What* else?"

"Don't know, unless we go and see."

"This here another hunch like the last? The one as led you to find Ben as the U. P. bandit?"

"Mighty like." Boyle gave a wolfish grin.

"Then, I say, do her! I'll run, tell Strom." The big man lumbered his bulk off toward the others.

Boyle eased the custom Smith and Wessons in their hand-tooled holsters. He nursed the feeling that he'd be getting his money's worth. Soon.

The coiled menace that was the timber rattler buzzed and struck, and struck hard. Ben Whitlow had attempted to rein the Circle Bar roan aside, but it was too late. The big snake had been in the middle of the trail, hurrying in the direction of a sunny flat rock, now that the rain was past. But the fugitive was in a hurry, too. The gelding's off foreleg was struck twice rapidly, and as the reptile whipped to cover, the terrified whinny rose to echo off the lofty rock ramparts. The horse reared, pawing, and the rider felt the saddle twist. Then he hurtled through the air and into the clear.

Ben Whitlow hit the ground with a solid thud and rolled. Above, the doomed animal, nostrils flaring, screamed and whirled. Its mouth frothing and eyes bulging, the roan bucked once, then stiffened and fell.

After that, it didn't take long. Whitlow watched the animal's final gasps in sheer frustration. There was a mighty shuddering, and then all was still.

In the birch and sycamores that flanked the cliffs, birds flitted and called. Across an open belt a nervous jackrabbit bolted, its tail flashing. By all rights, these wilderness signs should have lifted the heart of the man who'd just left a cell behind—but now he was in another fix.

There was only one thing that he considered fortunate, and that was the nearness of the hole-up canyon. He was at its very mouth now. Through a notch, and he'd be inside, free. He'd go on foot, of course, with nothing to lose.

Now he jammed the Walker Colt deeper in his waistband, and smoothed his fire red brush. He started moving at a tenderfooted upslope lope. He was confident he'd get through this if he could survive a few more days. And he would. His luck *had* to turn.

He didn't look up into the new cobalt cloudless sky. . . . or note the gathering of high, dust-speck buzzards above.

Chapter Fourteen

"Well, Zack Tree," Milt Henley said, "seeing as how them others ain't around no more, maybe we can get to swapping old yarns."

Tree stopped there in the street outside the doctor's office and fixed the bounty hunter with a blank stare. "Like we was real true friends?"

"Oh, come on. Ain't we? Hell, didn't I stick up for you in there, 'bout being the justice-bent hangman? Help the sawbones decide to spill out what he knew?"

The sun had wedged its way through the parting clouds, and it seemed the bad weather had lifted at last. A swallow veered past, landing on the jailhouse roof—and the jail reminded Tree all too sharply of Ben Whitlow. He'd managed to gain information from the medical man. And it was time to put it to use. But now

Milt Henley was in the picture, for better or for worse.

Tree shook his head and half smiled. "You done what you done because you guessed the doc's soft spot, and you might use any information yourself. You're a bounty hunter first and last, Henley. You want your money for buying gals like Rita-Sue and drinking."

Henley's grin was broad, but he still looked sinister. The mark of the long-past fight would ride over his eye always. "Hell, Zack, I know we've had our run-ins. But you helped me out in that fight. Them Slocums couldn't win, but I'd have got scraped up. So I figure I owe you." As the men walked, the tall one nudged the one in black. "You're backing this Ben Whitlow all the way, ain't you? I'll help you out."

A sidelong glance. "Oh?"

"Don't really need the bounty this time. Still flush from nailing Pigeon-Toed Sam."

Tree hesitated no further. "Teamwork'll be a help, I reckon." A few terse words, and he'd told Henley about the Van Aalsts.

"This banker's wife, you suspicions she helped Ben from the calaboose?"

"The doc's description fits. The woman's husband treats her bad. I'd like to test my hunch."

"I'll scare the truth out of her."

"I got a better way."

"I'll go in, jaw some with her alone," Tree told the bounty hunter as they neared the Van

Aalst mansion. "If things go like I want, we'll be needing broncs."

"Still riding the black gelding?"

"Roy's livery."

"Meet you there in a half hour."

A few rapid knocks brought the blond woman to her door. She opened up, looking flustered and surprised. "You? Here again? Oh dear! What—?"

"I'm guessing that this time your husband ain't to home. Ma'am, whether you care to or not, we got to palaver."

"Yes. Step inside, please." In her expression was none of the former hostility he'd seemed to fan, and he thought he knew why. If she had been Ben Whitlow's lover, it was natural she'd hate the man brought to hang him. But at their last meeting she'd caught a glimmer of the truth.

The hangman decided in the entryway to hit the Van Aalst woman hard and fast with it. "I know what your husband don't know about you and the condemned man. The only thing I don't understand, quite, is why you let him be found guilty at his trial."

"Good God! You've guessed?" Her dimpled cheeks had gone all pallid as she turned toward the fireplace.

"Not guessed without no clue. You were seen passing Ben the gun for his break."

"Morgan—"

"No, you don't got to fret about your husband. Word won't get around, leastways not from me and my friend. I found out from things Ben and

Caleb told me, and what a feller named Buster said before he died. Ben was with a gal the night of the big train holdup and killings. That his alibi should be plumb tight. But that he was protecting the gal—that was you, Mrs. Van Aalst. . . ." He paused solemnly. "How you could let his neck stretch just to protect your reputation?"

She spun, hands to her head, skirts aswirl. Then she faced him again, her blue eyes haunted. "Mr. Tree, you don't understand! Not my reputation, but my very life was at stake, and still is! Morgan Van Aalst is a violent man! He swore to kill me if I ever . . ."

"A feller like that, jealous? He might fear the law, but in this particular case—"

"His own vicious brother is the law! There was nothing to hold Morg back. I realized it. Ben was well aware, too. Ben insisted—he's sweet and noble. And in my mind's eye I planned helping his escape."

Zachariah Tree scratched his thatch of sorrel hair, and adjusted the wide-brim. He leaned against the brass cupid for a minute, thinking. "All right, the picture's come clear. Mrs. Van Aalst—"

"Josie."

"Josie, then. Josie, I'm betting you're still in love with the galoot, and want to help him even today."

"But he's gone, hightailed the territory. I'll be joining him in the Idaho camps as soon as Morg gives me next month's household allowance."

"If the plans you made pan out. And even then, the law might track Ben down anytime. But what if he didn't or couldn't rabbit across the Yellowstone? What if he's hereabouts yet, and the posse's like hounds on an elk's heels? What the feller needs is a cleared name, Josie. If I can locate him, I can likely help."

"So, you came to me. But his whereabouts, I don't—Wait a second! There's a place, a place we, er, were, together, more than once. A small box canyon on his ranch. I'll lead you there!"

Tree's grin was genial. Now he was getting somewhere. "If it's all the same to you, Josie, me and an *amigo* I'm teamed up with can ride harder on our own. So if you'll simply pass directions?"

It didn't take long, and Tree was exiting, heading for Roy's livery barn in long, distance-eating strides.

Roy had put the bounty hunter up on a deep-chested steel-dust, and the big horse showed its bottom keeping up the pace set by Tree as they rode hard out of town. The hangman's gelding, galloped easily to put the town behind. After more than an hour going parallel to the iron ribbons of the U. P. rails, the riders found themselves at what had been described as the holdup site. At the crest of a long grade there was a clutch of boulders, some huge, some small, and on the evening of the twenty-eighth, outlaws had blocked the right of way.

But what the law had cared about, mostly, was the stolen gold and the three slain guards.

The express car damaged when the safe had been blown was long since hauled away, but scars on the land remained. "This them?" Henley said, reining close to the embankment ruts. "Saw it from the eastbound, but then paid it no mind."

"Got to be," Tree concurred. "You say you paid no mind? Ain't it a bounty hunter's business, such?"

"Zack, on my way to Red Bluff, I had no hint you were the hangman involved. Heard about Whitlow's jailbreak from the telegraph man in Cheyenne and came to earn me the reward. I gave him a gold piece for the tip."

"Just another manhunt?"

"Your name sure weren't in the reward notice."

"I don't want it to be."

The man in black gigged his mount, angling for the distant peaks. Josie Van Aalst had outlined a far trek to the canyon hideout.

They rode for a good long while in silence, the mounts gobbling the miles, and the landscape greatly changing. Undulating ridges gave way to taller hills, and then they were pushing the black and the steel-dust along rugged trails, worn by game in a high-badlands maze. Climbing, ever climbing, they went from exposed cliffs to pockets girdled by pine. Then, at last, they were at the foot of a massive granite spire, a rushing stream ahead.

"Recognize it?"

Henley stroked his scarred brow. "From the woman's description you passed along."

"Back of the gap, Josie claimed, lays the canyon hideout. But look yonder." Tree pointed.

A buzzard dropped behind the rise.

"Buzzards tend to be where they're needed," Henley stated flatly. "Something's dead up there."

Simultaneously, the men whipped their mounts with their rein ends. They touched spur, and the horses lunged upslope in all-out runs.

The fat man descended from the day coach to the platform, while up the line the engine belched and brayed and took on water from the elevated tank. Across the tracks a few barefoot boys stopped whittling with their clasp knives, and gave a look. Just another flap-jowled jasper in a loud, checked suit. Little interested, next they tried mumblety-peg. "Hey, looka th' funny-face feller," one called out. "I seen littler stomachs on a family-way buff'lo!" "A thinner haunch on my uncle's prize hog!" "And less hair than a hard-boiled egg!"

Rufus Korthaller merely laughed and clutched his satchel's handle tighter in his pudgy grip. If he knew nature, those brats were on the path from mischief to downright crime. Give them time, and they'd wind up under his auspices. Swinging from a rope. Pissing, shitting, choking.

Rufus Korthaller sold mementos on the side: culprits' clothing scraps, bits of rope. Turning a pretty penny while the victims just turned.

"Haw! Now, where at's the eating 'stablishment?"

An older lady nearby swung her head away, a younger one stared straight past him. The drummer who'd shared his seat gestured down the street—and then fled the other way.

Rufus Korthaller waddled the main street like a colossus, ignoring the boardwalk, enjoying the looks of those forced to rein aside. Apparently it had rained lately—he splashed on through a puddle. Nice thing, rain. Didn't get much of it over in Nevada.

Markham's Delmonico had the largest sign in sight that proclaimed Hot Victuals, so Korthaller turned straight in as soon as he reached it. Inside, neat check-clothed tables were arranged in rows. There were few customers, but that could mean high prices as easily as poor food. The hefty hangman never cared much about the cost of meals; he earned enough from his profession and his sideshow income to eat and drink as he pleased.

"Hey, goddamnit, waiter, let's have us a peck o' service!" he whooped at the top of his lungs. A slouch-backed fellow in an apron ran in with a slate and chalk. The only other patron, a dandy with a waxed mustache, pushed his pie aside to watch.

"This the bill of fare on this here slate?" A nod. "Then fetch me the calf's-head soup, teal duck with sauce, and timbly of macaroni."

"Duck's all gone."

"Then the leg of mutton. Caper sauce."

"Wine?"

"An Old Overholt julep."

"Yessir."

At the front-corner table of Red Bluff's most extravagant restaurant, the Chronicle's Jethro Randolph bided his time.

Finally, when the waiter had poured the last fill of coffee for the fat man and hustled off with the empty plates, the newspaper made his move. Randolph rose hesitantly from his own table and minced toward Korthaller's, his round eyes wide and staring. The hefty hangman set his cup down, burped loudly, and sucked his fingers. The slack, round face oozed satisfaction from every pore.

"Er, pardon me, mister, I'm Jethro Randolph of the Chronicle. Unless these eyes deceive, Red Bluff's got 'em a celebrity in their midst. Ain't that right?"

Korthaller peered up, beaming as he sweated.

"I do believe I seen your picture in the public press, sir, more than once. Harper's Weekly, ain't it so? Or Scribner's Monthly?

"My repute, I gather, has traveled beyond the humble West."

"Then it's true! I'm face to face with Adolph Crantheller—"

"Rufus Korthaller!"

"Well, yes, of course." After the briefest of blinks, Randolph dropped into a chair. "Mr. Korthaller, sir, for the benefit of the press, can you say what's brought you to our town? You're a noted hangman, second in fame to perhaps only—"

"Ahem!"

"Sir?"

"No need to utter my rival's name. The fact is, Mr. Reporter, I've been sent for by your fair city's committee to replace the man. Seems he's failed to do his job. Stalled the stringing-up of the culprit Ben Whitlow. Claims to have a scruple that the condemned ain't guilty, really. Sir, a disgrace to the code!"

"Code?"

"Hangman's code: 'Swing 'em, no questions asked!'"

"I see." The Chronicle's best had out a pencil stub, scribbling in a notebook to beat the band. "Zack Tree discredited. Place taken by a different hangman." The girlish man slammed the book. "News, indeed. Now I'll be running off to set it up in type. Maybe this calls for an extra edition. . . ." Randolph strode off mumbling, bumping into chairs.

Korthaller heaved his bulk up and followed leisurely in Jethro Randolph's footsteps, pausing beside the door out to the street, at a small display in a front window. There was a plate with a slice of cake—yesterday's cake—butter pound cake, all the same. It had spent the night on the plate on the narrow stand. And an eating establishment naturally attracted flies.

Now an enormous bluebottle winged sluggishly upward from the coagulated frosting and soared off with a droning buzz. Rufus Korthaller reached out and popped the cake hunk between smacking lips.

Fly specks and all.

Chapter Fifteen

The beetling brow of rock that had caught the possemen's eyes now loomed above the party. They rode the canyon depths at a brisk, quick trot.

Two hard-riding days in the rough country they'd been combing, half of it in rain, had taken a toll. Excitement cooled. Hankering for home, the men sat their mounts and slipshodly spurred. A posse in this condition could only gain doubts—and not all connected with things told by leaders, loud or quiet.

"Whoa up!" called Boyle, his clenched right fist signaling. "Water here at this stream. Grab your smokes, men, if you've a mind. But we'll be pressing on in about ten minutes. Get your bladders empty and your cut-plug chawed."

Hans Mueller wrapped rough tradesman's

hands in his reins and swung down like the others.

"Boyle, you do know how to handle men," Mueller heard the sheriff say. The detective simply nodded and dusted off his twill pants with fringed gloves. The great big stallion with the black mane and tail thrust its muzzle in the water, and drank in noisy gulps. All up and down the sloped bank it was the same: horses drinking, men filling canteens. Under the cottonwoods' umbrella of shade it felt cool. Mueller finished filling his stomach, and sat on the sparse green grass. He plucked a stem to thrust between his teeth, and considered this mission.

He'd been one of the carpenters on the gallows job. Enjoyed the work. Now he wasn't so sure. He'd heard the rumors that old Caleb Whitlow's alibi for his son was sound, that most likely Ben Whitlow hadn't pulled a trigger, at the train holdup or afterward.

At the sound of the conversation, the German immigrant lifted his head. Three of them were talking: Van Aalst, Boyle, and a short, stocky, swarthy man Hans had seen around Red Bluff; Toot Satterlee.

"All right, fellers," the railroad dick said, uncovering his pewter gray head of hair. "By God, we ain't going to let Whitlow get back to town when we run him down. First we shoot, get all the possemen to open fire. Why put Red Bluff to the bother of a hanging at all? Now, when we can do the jasper's killing with our own guns. Man's condemned anyway."

Toot Satterlee said nothing, only bobbed his lank-haired, oblong noggin. Cain Van Aalst remarked, "Back shot, front shot, makes no nevermind. He left fair play behind when he pulled stakes out of jail."

"Well, he won't see the inside of a cell again. Right, Toot?"

"Right." The little man's tone was positive.

"Me," the sheriff said, "I'll cure Deputy McGraw to the plan."

"Er, 'scuse me, Sheriff?" Drawing close, Hans Mueller saw he was of a head with Satterlee. But of course, Satterlee wore chest-crossed shell belts and that brace of blued-steel Colts.

The lawman's neck swiveled. "Mueller, didn't notice you. What the hell—"

"Mebbe . . ." The German hoped his thick accent didn't put the men off. He had things to say. "Mebbe you, him"—he indicated the dick—"Mr. Boyle, there, mebbe you make a mistake. Mebbe that man Whitlow, he is not guilty. Mebbe should have new trial."

"Aw!" Cain Van Aalst inspected the star pinned to his vest, found it secure, slapped his six-gun butt, and turned to the horse waterers. "Time's up, men! Get ready to hit your goddamned saddles. Keep your guns unlimbered, case we spot the varmint! Remember, the reward says dead or alive!"

"B-but, Sheriff . . ." In the confusion of creaking leather, rattling bridle chains, and stamping hooves, the carpenter was ignored. He stood openmouthed, but mute as more than twenty heavily armed men swung aboard their mounts. And all the posse members were checking their rifles' and pistols' loads. All carried grim faces masked with forbidding, angry frowns. Mueller raced to a flat boulder, scrambled on it, snatched off, and waved his battered slouch hat. "Men! Listen to me!"

Up on the edgy *paso fino*, Rex, Justin Boyle locked eyes with Satterlee and shook his head. Wiry Toot Satterlee gave a single nod, and refrained from mounting up. With the clatter of hooves on rocks, the posse lined out and moved from under the trees and up across the next slanting, conical ridge.

Now Hans Mueller would need to hustle to catch up. He hastened to the converted farm plug he had been straddling, and laid a hand on the tuft-patched, shaggy hide.

The last of the possemen wended from sight. "You! Mueller!"

"*Ja?*"

"Want a word with you. Courtesy of Justin Boyle."

"*Ja?*"

The squat, square man with the barrel chest and thick arms moved scorpion-quick. With a step he closed in to fasten the German's coat front. Vise-gripping, he hauled the other man around.

"*Nein,* Mr. Satterlee! *Nein!* I only—"

Satterlee's fist was big for the rest of him. It came around now in a looping, upward drive. It connected hard with the solar plexus of the immigrant. Hans Mueller bent in the middle like a hinge.

"Filthy kraut!" Another vicious blow drove in to the kidneys. Lancing pain drove the German into an alder trunk. Satterlee's full-booted kick missed Hans's groin, but plowed his thigh with a numbing impact. Mueller pitched onto his belly, floundering in agony. Another slam of the leather-clad toe, and he heard gristle in his nose crackle like wadded paper. Metallic-tasting blood flooded his mouth from the jarred-loose teeth and cut gums. His vision was smeared with a fiery red haze.

"Learn ya!" Toot Satterlee danced back and forth, his thick, drooling lips curled in a devilish grimace. Now he drove his hand down with a full-armed slash to the immigrant's exposed ear. Mueller shouted with the pain, only to have the shout cut off. Satterlee had snatched up a rock, held it over the German, and stood poised for a split second. Then he arced the projectile downward with all his force, glancing it against the bleeding, twitching face.

Hans Mueller's body bucked, went rigid, then completely limp. Gouts of blood continued to pump from his nostrils, ears, and mouth, but there were no more grunts, no screams. Satisfied, Toot Satterlee wrung his scuffed-up hands. A lot of the punishment had been absorbed by the rugged pigskin gloves he'd donned. Now he stepped from the downed man to his bronc, a hammerheaded skewbald with a mangy mane.

He put his boot in the stirrup, and swung lightly aboard.

His heart, such as it existed, was light, too. He always felt better after victory in a fight. And he'd have a good one to report to the bossman, sure as "furriners" felt pain.

Yeah, Justin Boyle had done a lot for Toot Satterlee in the few months since he'd gotten out of territorial prison in Montana and joined his team.

Deputy Ike McGraw spied them first, dropping out of the indigo dusk sky beyond the ridge, and he yelled out to Justin Boyle and the possemen around him: "Buzzards, by God! Something's wrong for somebody or some critter! Head that way?"

"You bet," called the man with the blade nose, head of pewter hair, and crisp new Stetson. "Guns at ready, men, now as we advance! Could be, that killer polecat Whitlow's laid an ambush. Blast the first glimpse of him y'all catch! I want him pumped full of hot lead!"

"You heard the man," Sheriff Cain Van Aalst affirmed. "Let's go!"

The loose group of riders bunched to a swarm at the signal, galloping up the fold of ground and over the ridgetop. As they thundered across, they were among whipping, slashing saplings, and then through the belt and breaking down into the saucer of a notch. They suddenly came upon the stiff, dead horse as it lay across their path, legs thrust at awkward angles, disgustingly carrion torn. Dozens of the ugly, gore-smeared buzzards flopped away and took to the air with a harsh beat of their giant wings. The few that remained huddling among the jumbled boulders simply stared balefully. Boyle signaled the halt.

"Whoa! Whoa up!"

Toot Satterlee reined the skewbald beside the noble *paso fino* of his pard. "That's the bronc stole from in front of the Bijou! See the Circle Bar brand?"

"Whitlow's nearby!"

Boyle dragged his Winchester from its saddle boot. He jacked a cartridge into the chamber with a practiced motion. Satterlee already wielded his Colts.

"Are you ready, fellers? We spread out now and comb back of them there—"

A croak burst from Cain Van Aalst's mouth. "Wait a goddamn minute! Something's coming through the clump of greasewood!"

"Hold your fire, men!" Abraham Strom roared out lustily.

"Jesus Christ," Satterlee blurted.

Through the break in the undergrowth moved two straddled horses, a black and a leggy steel-dust gray. The steel-dust carried double.

"Hello, the posse," shouted Zachariah Tree, kneeing the black mount to bring it between the fugitive and the row of leveled guns.

"Tree, get your ass outta the line of fire!"

Abraham Strom shouted, beet faced: "Men of Red Bluff! Hold your fire! Hold your fire!"

The group and the trio trotted their mounts cautiously toward each other, meeting in the center of the glade under towering limestone and sandstone heights. "Sheriff. Boyle." Tree nodded curtly to both men in the lead, at the same time raking his cool, gray gaze over the townsmen drawn up in the rear. "Here's your prisoner, who me and Milt Henley, here, found and talked into giving himself up. It's our word," he added meaningfully, "that's been gave, he'll make it back to town alive. Not shot in the back, you understand, whilst 'resisting arrest.'"

"You got your nerve, Tree, dictating—"

"Sheriff, if we cut the talk and ride, we'll be back at Red Bluff by dinner instead of breakfast."

"All right, all right. Our rumps are as tired as yours. Mind if some of the boys ride behind? I ain't betting much on Whitlow's honor, do you see?"

"Understandable, Sheriff. Understandable."

Horses stamped and danced, half-spooked by the dead mount, but finally the troop moved on out and back along the rock-strewn route they'd come. Tree judged the distance to Red Bluff as three hours' worth of hard riding.

The scowling Justin Boyle calculated the same.

Ben Whitlow hissed to Henley, "They were

156

set to gun me down, sure. I'm grateful you found me first. Beholden to have my bacon saved."

"It ain't all saved quite yet," husked the bounty hunter. "Not if you're still feared of bringing in Mrs. Van Aalst. You got another enemy in town, could be your end, and a pretty bad end."

Whitlow glanced across to Tree. The hangman compressed his tight lips. "Name's Rufus Korthaller."

Chapter Sixteen

"I'll do Whitlow tonight after sunset, by torch-light," Korthaller said, glancing around the office of the jail and yawning.

Cain Van Aalst's face was slack with fatigue. Last night's ride out of the hills beyond the Double W spread had left him with a mere two hours of sleep and a headache big as the whole Rocky Mountain front range. He'd have no patience with further delay of brash Ben Whitlow's execution. So the condemned jasper was in a windowless cell, manacled.

Zachariah Tree, God blast his ornery hide, was due in the worst way for some comeuppance.

"Just a piebald, shit-and-be-damned minute, Korthaller," the sheriff blurted in a building fury. "You're here on hand to act as hangman, the scaffold's all up, and the damned town's ready as it'll be! Me"—he thumped his chest—"him—" The gesture took in Justin Boyle, sitting in Van Aalst's hard chair. "We plumb ain't inclined to wait for what's past cooking time and fuming! And as for them"—Tree and Henley, lounging by the spare-gun cabinet—"they got nothing at all to say! I demand a hanging this very morning! About an hour from now!"

Rufus Korthaller's Ingram pocket timepiece was in his plump palm. "Out of the question. It's only half past seven. I ain't even had my eye-opener yet. A stone fence, that there's cider and brandy."

Van Aalst failed to flinch at the concoction's description. "I don't care if it's goat piss mixed with vinegar! By God—"

"Take me time to get ready." The fat man mopped his sweaty dome.

"You been in town all night!"

"Catching up on rest."

"Brought prepared rope with you?"

He yawned. "Lariat stock, but—"

"I reckon I see our new hangman's point of view," Boyle interrupted. "He wants the best job possible. That means the chance to prepare. Even Tree saw the need for the like when the task was his, before he had his second notions. Right, Tree?"

"Right."

"Thought so."

"One place we agree."

Boyle bowed without getting up, his face

twisted in a devilish smile. "Professional courtesy—"

"Christ! Enough's enough!" The town's chief lawman, Van Aalst took a quick turn around the small open area. Drew his thick potbellied bulk up in front of the railroad dick. "Boyle, if you want to give Korthaller time, then you're giving Tree and the bounty hunter time. They're out to clear Whitlow, they admit it. If they come up with proof about the robbery, the train—"

"There ain't no proof!" Justin Boyle was on his feet and lurching forward. He shook his fist at Tree. "No proof, Tree, no alibi for your man that'll stick! No capture of the gang that got away! Even if the stole money turns up, young Ben Whitlow swings, kicks his life away, his neck stretched in a tight noose!"

Toe to toe with Zack Tree, the livid railroad dick stood. His expensive clothes were soiled with trail dirt and rain. The Smith and Wessons could use an oiling, the same with the silver-mounted spurs. Justin Boyle needed a shave; the stubble across the long, cleft chin was a dirty gray smear. "You may's well get out of Red Bluff now, Tree," he stormed. "Too bad you and the bounty hunter got the right to wait for the company's reward money." He spun, and with a jingle of the spurs, stalked out the open door.

Milt Henley shrugged. Zachariah Tree shrugged.

Rufus Korthaller dug at his crooked dark teeth with a golden toothpick. He pocketed the pick abruptly. "Gents, I'm off to breakfast. Delmonico's for an hour. Then, find me at the *Chronicle*. Got some printing work to arrange with Mr. Randolph. Fine fellow, he. Not unwilling to be dickered down in his rates."

"We got to be going, too, Milt," Tree observed. The man with the scarred brow shoved away from the wall.

"Right. Got to get a mite of sleep."

"Milt, we got ten hours or more."

"Lucky Korthaller is being a lazy slug."

Zack Tree grinned. "Ain't you seen through that faking son of a bitch? He wants a long hanging day so's to take more profit. Selling the crowd handbills with Ben's story printed. Plus the saloons give him a cut of their bonanza take."

The morning sun was bright, and they were squinting. The bounty hunter licked his dry lips. "*All* the watering holes? All pay the fat jasper?"

"Likely."

"Then, which one'll we be taking ourselves to?"

"Didn't have us luck last time at the Silver Slipper, would you say, Milt? Make it the Bijou, then."

The pair sat opposite the bar at a scarred and scored round side table in the saloon, under the big pink painting of the naked lady. The main light at this time of morning were the mote-ridden rays from the windows at the front. Tree nursed a beer; Milt Henley nursed one, too.

Tree built a quirly and lit it. Henley's squint eye closed still further at the strong and pungent smoke.

"We never brought the kid back for no reward."

"No. But let Boyle think we're staying in town so's to collect."

"Keep the son of a bitch off guard? Zack, your rope's run out. How in hell you aim to clear young Whitlow any more? I don't see the real train robbers coming forward. Likely they're in Californy, whoring fit to bust."

Tree drank, then puffed and exhaled a smoke ring.

"Wait a minute. You hear Boyle say he wants us out of Red Bluff, but we got a right to wait around for the reward from the U. P. railroad. Milt, the railroad put up no reward, not for getting back the loot, not for Ben Whitlow's capture. Dispatcher told me that over drinks in the Silver Slipper."

One of Milt Henley's long, soft whistles. "Badger in the woodpile!"

"Looks that way. So who is around to pony up hard cash?"

"Reckon it's the real outlaws, else their boss. Once Ben Whitlow's in the grave, there's no risk that he'll slither his way to get cleared. Then the robbery doings can be laid to rest, a goat made to pay for the murders." Henley slapped the table-top. "Yeah!" But next—" His mouth turned down. "Zack, it don't play. Why'd Boyle, of all people, go along with owlhoots?"

"Keep thinking."

"Boyle himself's the bossman? But, he's a railroad dick! Done busted his ass to bring in Ben Whitlow—"

"Union Pacific men, they got access to train schedules, the shipments as gets made. That goes for payroll shipments, too. The bandits vanished in the hills, tracks lost on rocky ground. Next day, Boyle's in Red Bluff, and he goes out alone, brings back—guess who?"

"Boyle's sworn word at Ben's trial woulda been enough to fool a jury of the dead guards' friends."

"Right as rain." Tree smiled grimly.

"But it still don't wash. Boyle wired for Korthaller."

"Who'd be Boyle's sidekicks? The sheriff?"

"The sheriff is Morg Van Aalst's brother. Unlikely he'd risk the banker's shipment. Could ruin the Red Bluff bank."

A glitter gal had drifted close to the conferring men. She looked haggard as hell. "Let us alone," the bounty man snapped flatly.

She found other things to do.

"No," Tree continued, "not the sheriff, nor any solid citizen of the town. Train holdup, that's gunslicks' work. Remember, Milt, I told you I got bushwhacked?"

"When the cowhand Buster got shot, yeah. You killed the sniper."

"One of two snipers. The other rabbited."

"But, goddamnit, Zack, there ain't no scrap of proof!"

Tree snorted. "Not for lawmen or courts, no. But we got us more sense than courts. Real justice sense! Listen. Who rides a *paso fino* stud? Who packs handmade S and W Schofields? Wears tailored coats? Fifty-dollar Stetson?" He paused. "How much a U. P. detective earn?"

"Not enough."

"That ties it."

The bounty man drained the dregs of his beer and slammed the glass down. "What can we do, Zack? We can't break Ben loose again—the whole town's on the alert now."

Over in the far corner, a forlorn whore was plinking the piano. Now and then she sang a note or a couple—disastrously off key. Tree told Milt Henley: "Time to be clearing out of this place. The gal sounds like a scalded cat."

"You ain't forgetting Ben Whitlow's appointment with the hangman Korthaller?"

"No, I got me a plan to flush a lobo from his den." He jammed his hat down tightly. "Tell you on the way to the livery stable."

"The way I see it, Boyle," Milt Henley said, "agreeable to it or not, you got to listen to me." He sat on the bed in the railroad cop's room in the Colorado Hotel, thinking the layout unworthy of the name. A stained bureau stood next to a crowded standing wardrobe against a wall done in striped, peeling paper. Behind the one chair sat a cracked, rose-petal-figured thunder mug.

Justin Boyle slouched inches from the door, his lean hands held inches from his six-guns. His face was angry, staring at the bounty hunter. The silvery hair almost bristled.

With a damnable coolness the visitor fished in a trouser pocket, and brought out a clasp knife with which he pared his fingernails.

Boyle waited.

Henley pared.

Standoff.

"I got me a notion, Detective," Henley said. "Came on this morning. The kind of idee a feller with empty pockets gets. Else, one that's greedy. *Amigo*, you catch my drift?"

"Go on."

"Now, you'll say I got title to the reward money for that sad son of a bitch, Whitlow. But that's got to get split with Tree, leaving this child with a poor seven hundred and fifty. Not enough for a feller with a taste for gambling, whiskey, gals. Now, a cut of a train-holdup take, on the other hand—"

"What the goddamn hell—?"

"Hear a feller out." Still cutting his finger-nails with concentration, the sinister bounty man spoke calmly, not looking at the railroad dick. "The notion as come, it's this. Ben Whitlow didn't rob the U. P., didn't give no guards lead poisoning. For sure, he'd of never run and hid at his own ranch. So that part of *your* story,

Boyle, is a bushel of lies, packed down and mounded over. Now the question is, why'd the big, important detective set up somebody innocent to take the blame? Except maybe that the detective was in on the job himself? Likely its leader, on account of his information on when the shipments come and go?"

"You call me a liar, Henley? When you—"

The bounty man smoothed an extra-tricky bit of nail. "My notion explains the fancy stud horse you own. The costly duds, too. Those ain't explained in no other way. But let me come to the point. I want half your loot stash, understand? Half. So you maybe paid off your sidekicks, maybe not. That's why I'm naming no figure." He glanced up from his paring at last. "Me and you, we're going to ride out to your money cache. It can't be far, so we'll do it pronto, now."

Boyle dropped his hands.

"Don't try for them hoglegs! What'll gunplay in the hotel do? Draw folks, make you a suspicious party? Can you afford that?"

"I can afford having you dead, mister."

"If you could beat me to the draw, and even if'n you did, then even Van Aalst would need to ask what was between you and me. No, I got to go on living. You won't do me in now, Boyle. You'll make us pards instead."

"Me and you and . . . Tree?" His look was shifty as a monte thrower's hands.

"Tree ain't in this. Ain't enough gold to go around." Henley snapped the little knife closed.

"I'll fetch your share back to you here."

"Like the bluebellies keep injun treaties!" Henley, on his feet now, moved for the door, jauntily tossing his clasp knife, catching it . . . *Missing* it! The little device of steel and gutta-percha slipped from his extended fingers, bounded away and to the floor.

Henley dropped to his knees, clawing for the knife.

Justin Boyle drew his right-hand six-gun, and brought it around and down toward the bent bounty hunter's skull. The Smith and Wesson's barrel hit Milt just above his ear. But even in the off-balance, low position, the bounty hunter moved his right arm with speed like a deadly rattlesnake's. The long Remington .44 factory conversion seemed to leap into his hand, and it came up cocked and pointed at the railroad dick's flat nose.

Justin Boyle froze.

"Now, I reckon we know who's the better gunslick, don't we, U. P. backstabber? But I reckon I won't kill you, on account of I still want that cut of your stole gold. You done playing? Then holster your toy. We got us a ride ahead of us."

They went down the hotel's rear stairs and out the back door.

Henley had put up his six-gun, too, but he kept his hand close to the well-worn walnut grip.

Chapter Seventeen

Pushing the black gelding hard, Tree followed the steel-dust and the *paso fino* stud. The hangman was keeping well back along the open stretches and making use of any concealment offered by broken terrain. The plan was to remain unseen by Boyle, if not by the bounty hunter. He could only hope Henley was still working his plan. In any case, as the riders ahead made their run to reach the U. P. loot, things looked better than they had from the first for saving Ben Whitlow from the noose.

Toward late morning they were angling across a high, sage-patched tableland. By noon they had dropped down again into a maze of gullies and small canyons, mostly undergrowth choked, yet offering a distinct and traveled trail.

But as Tree came around a jumbled rubble of

fallen rimrock, the clear trail disappeared. Ahead lay another changed stretch of ground marked by firs, boulders, and a frothing stream. In the miles behind, Tree had closed the distance gap between himself and his quarry, and so had managed to keep the other men in sight. Now the hangman would need to rely on tracking the deep hoofprints in the soft earth.

The *paso fino's* hoof marks were easy to spot, thanks to Roy the liveryman's file work on an off-rear horseshoe.

Then, crossing a rise, Tree glanced to his own rear, and what he saw brought a curse to his lips.

Back there—well back—were the dust plumes of two more riders. Riders apparently trailing *him*. This could spell a heap of trouble.

He urged the black horse down the far side of the ridge, and maintained a brisk lope across the flat and along the timbered base of the next cliff face. From there, he rode through a maze of shattered, giant granite chunks fallen from up top. Small, blooming plants carpeted the spaces between.

Tree's mind wasn't on beauty of scene, but on the danger he could be riding into. He'd felt his neck hairs crawl in warning, and the sensation was coming on strongly now. He rounded yet another of the trail's sharp jogs, finding himself uncomfortably in the open. But there was no other way to go and still stick with Boyle's and Henley's tracks.

He was just ten yards from a beech and elder

stand when the shout came. "Rein up! Hoist your hands, hangman! Now, stay put, and we'll hike out to you!"

Tree saw the cabin huddled under the overhang. It was old and tumbledown, with most of the roof fallen in, but the weathered logs still made a firm breastwork. Round holes of gun barrels peered from the one window.

Wordlessly, he raised his hands.

As soon as he'd done so, Boyle and Henley stepped into view. The men kept well apart as they advanced with weapons leveled. "Could've shot you stone dead from ambush," Boyle growled tersely. "It's what the bounty man wanted to do, but I thought better. I got to know something before you eat a bullet. You ride out all this way alone?"

Tree glanced at Henley, but the mustached face was as blank as a tombstone slab. "Matter of fact, Boyle, no, I wasn't such a fool as to come without pards. They're back of me on the trail, and'll be all over you like fleas, should a shot be fired here. Then I wouldn't give an empty hash tin for your chance of fighting clear with your loot. Killing the railroad guards and framing Ben will go for nothing."

"So you figured out what Henley figured out, too! By the way, he's come over to my side. Right now is his chance to prove it, cut his way in on the gold stashed in the cabin." He spoke to Henley from the corner of his mouth. "Well, I'm keeping my gun on him. Go on in and cut his throat with your Bowie."

A long minute passed, but finally Milt Henley took a step forward and then another.

"Go on ahead!"

But the show being played out was interrupted. The mountain stillness was cut suddenly by the rolling clatter of running horses' hooves. Off the rocky trail and onto the grass swale the two riders pounded, then pulled the animals to halts on their haunches.

Relieved, Tree grunted.

One rider, a squat, stocky jasper, Tree recognized from the posse. The other was Sheriff Cain Van Aalst.

"Glad you showed, Sheriff. Keep them two covered like you are. Boyle, there, he's the leader of the gang that hit the train, and the stolen gold is cached inside."

Over his unbooted Henry carbine, the lawman's pig eyes squinted and raked the men on foot. "Lucky me and Toot Satterlee got here when we did."

Henley burst out, "Boyle's your man, all right! He's done admitted! The hangman figured it, and we worked to trap the bastard—"

Van Aalst's rifle muzzle swung Tree's way, and the tin-star triggered. There was a bang, and bright flame speared. . . .

Morg Van Aalst's fist slammed Josie's face, and the woman was hurled with the force of the blow against the front wall of the parlor. The glass in the curtained bay window rattled, and a framed print of General U. S. Grant went crashing to the floor.

"Bitch! Slut!" The big man's shirtsleeved arm flexed another time as the woman rebounded, and sent the elbow sledging into her chest with pain that felt like fired lungs. She choked a faint scream, emitting blood spray as well as sound, then fell, sprawling beside a flower-printed carpetbag. "Set to walk out on old Morg? Lucky I happened home for lunch! Catched you red-handed! Who's th' other man, damn your eyes? Who?"

Her mouth pinched shut, and she shook her head. A purple mouse puffed out her cheek. Morg Van Aalst kicked at it. Connected. She wailed like scalded pup.

"Has to be a man! 'Member what I promised if you fooled me?" He moved to straddle her, reached, and hauled her to her feet. A ringing slap impacted against her face. The head jerked with a sickening snap. Now a constant groaning rose in her throat. He released Josie, and she hinged over and staggered backward, upsetting a low table.

"Swore you had to be mine only, leave off whoring! I'll wring your stringy neck!" He grabbed her throat.

She gagged, her brain fogged by a vivid crimson cloud. And then she couldn't see at all, and there was nothing but pain. She felt the vessels in her neck stretch, breaking. Tortured lungs fought in vain for air. Two fluttering hands, kitten weak, played across the husband's waist-

172

coat: smooth silk, rough embroidery. Then a lump. A vest pocket with a lump! Desperate fingers probed, found the fine-stitched slit.

"Good-bye, Josie, slut, good—"

She yanked the derringer clear, and fired it blindly. The report seared her ears, and suddenly she was free. She stumbled away, and the big form floated a moment, then toppled. Big Morg Van Aalst lay on the floor, a bloody hole in his chest.

Josie flinched at the sight, then her eyes raised from the fallen gun to the open door. A dark form filled the doorway, looming, and there was a smaller, bonneted form peering around its side.

"Passing in the street, heard the fracas," Jethro Randolph wheezed. "Don't fret none, little lady, I seen it was self-defense."

"Me, too," piped the widow Ann Johnson.

Josie Van Aalst's head felt strange. Her large blue eyes rolled back.

She collapsed in a faint.

Tree sidelonged, catapulting back, and the sheriff's slug whipped through his sleeve, grazing his forearm. The bolt of hurt that seared the hangman swept a curtain across his eyes. There was no time to stagger, not with Cain Van Aalst following him with that gun. Propelled by legs taut and strong as wagon springs, he threw himself into the lawman's stocky dun. Arms wrapped around the lawman's leg, he dragged the sheriff from his saddle.

The stout, swearing badge packer dropped on the ground, and Tree fell on him, knees first.

Satterlee tossed a shot at Henley, which kicked up a divot the size of a cow pie at his feet. The bounty man fired, hitting the bay Toot rode. The animal, shot in the neck, took a few crow-hopping steps to fall by Boyle. Satterlee bounded from the soft earth where he'd landed to dive in attack.

Henley triggered one Remington, then the other.

Satterlee somersaulted back, sprawled unmoving on the grass.

"Son-of-a-bitching double-crosser!" It was Boyle's turn to pile into the fight. Henley spun to face him.

Zachariah Tree drove a fist to the downed sheriff's chin. His rifle lost, the lawman was struggling to bring his Colt to bear. The hangman wrapped both hands together and brought them down hard on the enemy's wrist. The fingers sprang apart, and the pistol flew wide and wild. Cain Van Aalst, however, was a vicious brawler, and from somewhere inside his boot he produced a knife. A thrust with the wicked Arkansas toothpick narrowly missed Tree's neck.

At point-blank range, but hurrying their shots, Milt Henley and Boyle exchanged gunfire. Boyle's gleaming Schofield Models blazed, throwing fire and smoke. Henley returned shot for shot in the drifting gray cloud. The bounty hunter felt his hat plugged. A different slug tugged his shirt along the ribs. He ducked and rolled. All of a sudden, a waft of wind lifted, clearing things. Henley, on his belly, glimpsed the pewter gray thatch. Boyle crouched grinning, sheened with sweat. His gloved hands balanced his own twin .45's.

"Got you, bounty man! By my count, you're out of rounds!" His poised, coiled index fingers tightened. . . .

Reacting puma-quick, Tree flung himself from the sheriff and at Boyle. He knocked up the dick's triggering hands. The S and Ws exploded at the sky.

Henley leaped at the sheriff. One, two, three hard-knuckled raps to the lawman's mouth cut his lips and broke his teeth. The bounty hunter clawed his opponent by his neck bandanna and drew back his right fist for a mighty roundhouse blow.

"No more! I quit!" the sheriff whined.

Zack Tree brought up the miniature Captain Jack from his side and fired. The round hurtled into Justin Boyle's left shoulder, spinning him. He dropped both guns. And then Tree was at the railroad dick's side, jerking around his good arm, pinning it. "Fight's over, feller. You agree, or do I got to kill you where you stand?"

"Damn you, Tree, I give up."

"Good. Maybe we'll get to use those new gallows, after all." And turning to Henley, he said, "Thought you'd deserted to the enemy."

"Hell, I wouldn't do that, Zack. Not to you."

"Leastways not this time, hey?" To Cain Van Aalst he said, "So the sheriff was in on the holdup, too. And after your brother pinned that star on you, made life easy."

"I hate Morg's guts! Nose-in-the-air bastard!"

"Who's that one?" Henley was pointing at the corpse of Satterlee.

"Another of the gang? Watched at my rooming house? Bushwhacked Buster and me at the Whitlow's ranch? Why'd you order him and his pard to, Boyle? Peg me as trouble when I hit town?"

The railroad dick spat. "Screw you!"

Henley glanced up at the declining sun. "Speaking of Ben Whitlow . . ."

"We'll be in time to save him. Korthaller moves slow, but we won't. Help me tie these bastards to their broncs."

"The reward—?"

"No, the loot, all that's left, goes back to the railroad, Milt, old *compadre*." The hangman flashed a rare grin. "Don't your heart warm at your good deed?"

"Shit!"

Chapter Eighteen

The gallows reared tall, but cast virtually no shadow. The noon-hour sun baked down, and Red Bluff simmered in a high-plains wind that smelled of dust. The hanging apparatus had been improved on and expanded since the day Ben Whitlow sat sweating out his doom in jail. Now two trapdoors took the place of one. Now a long overhead beam held two ring bolts, and two nooses dangled, waiting.

The crowd in the street was orderly—so far. Chief town committeeman Abe Strom was on patrol, and his frowning glare for some reason kept the folks somber.

But things had been quieter than usual around Red Bluff ever since the young rancher had been declared innocent of involvement in the Union Pacific robbery, and his cell had been given to the two actual leaders of the vicious outlaw gang.

The men really responsible for the deaths of the express guards by cold-blooded Colt triggering were Justin Boyle and Cain Van Aalst. The very pair that the town had let itself be fooled by. The lawmen-turned-outlaws had received a quick trial and had been convicted. Some jurors claimed the loot found in the cabin swayed them. Others credited the finding of railroad guard Hube Johnson's gold watch under the dick's mattress.

Now men and women, young and old, stood shuffling on their feet, glancing at their own timepieces, mopping faces with hankies and sleeves. Hangman Tree had requested that the saloons be closed for an hour. The owners caved in without much squawk. There would be a land-office business done through the rest of the long day.

Just when the tension had grown unbearable, the wide door of the jailhouse flew open. The prisoners were marched out by armed committee members at a quick step. The pair were hustled up the raw scaffold steps and positioned on the raw-pine floor. A parson stroked his copy of the Good Book fussily. Then Zack Tree mounted the gallows steps, black coat and trousers brushed and freshly flatironed. Between the lapels his boiled and starched, spotless shirt gleamed a dazzling white. The string tie was carefully knotted.

"Any last words?"

Boyle and Van Aalst were tightly pinioned with stout chest straps, arm straps, and leg straps. They balanced on their feet, sometimes teetering. "Last words?" Boyle grunted.

"What in hell for?" The ex-sheriff defiantly spat.

"No objection to hoods, I reckon?" The hangman produced them from a pocket, fixed the black cloth blinders in place.

Silence gripped the area. It was as if all were holding long-pent-up breaths.

Tree briefly scanned the throng, caught no sight of Ben or Josie, or even Caleb. Then he recalled the rumor he'd heard: they had taken the morning train. They were to wed that very afternoon over in Cheyenne.

Too bad Korthaller had been summoned some days back for a job California way. Had he stuck around, he'd have learned something.

So might Henley, but he'd ridden for the Indian nations. A juicy reward was posted for the notorious Reno Kid.

The hangman slipped the nooses over the condemned men's hooded heads.

Now even the preacher's mumbling prayer was hushed. Tree put his right hand on the lever that controlled the traps, waited a moment, then jerked it down.

The traps dropped quickly, and the culprits fell through the gaping hole, helpless weights. Dead weights.

Snap!

The culprits swung for all to see through the open framework. Long-dropped, both had died in one split second. The fronts and rears of their trousers stained, they hung with necks stretched, motionless, but for slow twisting in the breeze.

A collective sigh erupted from the crowd. The green parson covered his gagging mouth, and hastened down the steps and away. Tree descended in a more leisurely fashion. When he was on the ground, he avoided a smiling gal bent on hailing him.

He nodded to the liveryman Roy.

"All right, Jason," Strom was telling the undertaker. "Hangman's orders are the corpses don't get cut down for an hour. Though this pair sure ain't walkin' no place!"

Tree rounded the coffin-laden parked hearse, and there she was: Mrs. Ann Johnson.

Her pinched, chalky lips opened. "Oh, Mr. Tree. I turned out to watch, not expecting it'd be so . . . so—"

"Awful?"

A tearful, hurried nod.

"It's why I take my job serious, like I do, ma'am. Once the nooses jerk, it's a bitter end."

He brushed past, frowning, and entered the jailhouse, where his worn leather traveling bag waited.

He plucked up the telegraph flimsy that he'd been handed just as he was stepping outside.

Tree peered casually through the window
and saw the crowd rapidly dispersing to saloons. Nevertheless, he used the back door as
being the easy way.

Five minutes later he was at the depot, dictating.

"Can I sell you a ticket, too, then?" the clerk
wanted to know.

When Zack Tree finds he's hanged innocent
men, he vows to find the real killer and see him
swing in the next exciting adventure:

#2: BLOOD KNOT